Henry S. Leigh

A Town Garland

A Collection of Lyrics

Henry S. Leigh

A Town Garland
A Collection of Lyrics

ISBN/EAN: 9783744787925

Printed in Europe, USA, Canada, Australia, Japan

Cover: Foto ©Andreas Hilbeck / pixelio.de

More available books at **www.hansebooks.com**

A

TOWN GARLAND.

A COLLECTION OF LYRICS.

BY

HENRY S. LEIGH,

AUTHOR OF " CAROLS OF COCKAYNE," ETC.

London:

CHATTO AND WINDUS, PICCADILLY.

1878.

𝔅𝔞𝔩𝔩𝔞𝔫𝔱𝔶𝔫𝔢 𝔓𝔯𝔢𝔰𝔰.
BALLANTYNE, HANSON AND CO.
EDINBURGH AND LONDON

To

FREDERICK LOCKER

𝕿𝖍𝖊𝖘𝖊 𝖁𝖊𝖗𝖘𝖊𝖘

are dedicated by his grateful admirer

THE AUTHOR.

PREFACE.

THIS is the third book of rhymes with which I have tried the patience of the public. My present volume, like my two previous ones, is composed of pieces that have already seen the light in various periodicals. However unsatisfactory the reader may pronounce them in a collected form, I trust that their brevity will preserve them from the charge of being separately tedious.

To those gentlemen who have given me the right of republication, I beg to convey hereby my sincere thanks.

H. S. L.

CONTENTS.

CONTENTS.

GOOD-BYE, MUSE!

(A VALEDICTORY INTRODUCTION.)

ADIEU to my pens—to my ink—to my paper—
 The slaves that enslaved me, to laugh me to
  scorn.
Farewell to the gas—to the oil—to the taper—
 That beamed on my vigil from darkness to morn.
Go, hang up my harp, like the mute one of Tara ;
 No more shall it throb to my lyric or lay ;
The pastures of rhyme are for me a Sahara,
 No more to be traversed by night or by day.

Oh, Muse ! oh, my private particular dear one ;
 In vain did I single thee forth from the Nine.
Thou never wilt answer—thou never wilt hear one—
 I never can hope for ten minutes of thine.
I seek not a gallop, I ask but a canter ;
 Say, where, oh, ye Muses, can Pegasus be ?—
While bards by the dozen may mount him *instanter*,
 He never stirs out of the stable for *me*.

A

My wish was to carol but lightly and gaily ;—
   To give to the crowd in its moments of mirth
Faint echoes of Praed and of Butterfly Bayly,
   And flutter my wings pretty close to the earth.
Our tribe never aims for the brow of Parnassus,
   We seek no refreshing from Castaly's rill ;—
Unheeding the great who mount upward and pass us,
   We stop to play games at the foot of the hill.

Farewell to ye, Muses ! I quit your dominion,
   I leave it this minute, and leave it for good ;
Meanwhile I may state, as my settled opinion,
   That none of ye treated me quite as ye *should.*
Some trade or department of commerce I'll follow,
   And fight for the pounds and the shillings and
      pence ;
And if I say, *Sic me servavit Apollo,*
   'Tis meant in the strictly ironical sense.

THE WIDOW AND HER BOY.

SHE mateless and the fatherless—upon the
world alone!
 Two dreamers o'er a happy past—a past for
ever flown.
No brightness has the day for *them*, no calmness has
the night;
For *them* the sunny summer-time no longer brings
delight.
Whene'er they take their walks abroad, how many
poor they see
Whose days are full of industry, whose nights are full
of glee!
What marvel that they mourn for *him*—he died not
long ago—
By whose decease the leather trade sustained so sad
a blow?

Some say 'tis forty blessed years, while some say
forty-five,
Since Edith S——, the widow'd one, began to be alive.

As good a judge of years am I as others claim to be,
And I consider Edith S—— exactly forty-three.
They hint that she is lowly born—they tell me she is
    fat—
They call her ugliness itself; she *is*, but what of that?
I plant my faith in dividends, my confidence in rents;
House property is *not* á dream, no more are Three
    per Cents.

We met—methinks 'twas in a crowd—a month ago
    and more.
Be still, my giddy heart, be still!—To see was to adore.
Enough, enough! I dare do all that may become a
    man;
But what was *I?*—A City clerk, with nothing much
    per ann.
Yet, warmed with wine and enterprise, I breathed my
    early love;
I swore by all the earth below and all the stars above.
She heard me.—Did she understand? Her face she
    coyly hid;
But, by the pressure of her hand, I rather think she
    did.

I told you, reader—did I not?—she had an only child:
A half-neglected thing of ten, intractable and wild.
Nay, "wild" is all inadequate—"intractable" is weak
To paint that soul of impudence, that prodigy of cheek.

I love to sport with little ones; I love the merry tricks
Of little boys or little girls of only five or six.
Their silly talk, their winning ways, amuse me now
    and then;
But if I hate one living thing, it is a boy of ten.

He calls me "poor old buffer," too, or words to that
    effect;
And when he cracks my spectacles, I own that I
    object.
Though little more than thirty-four, I'm growing rather
    bald,
But scarcely wish to hear the fact so pointedly
    recall'd.
He hides my hat, my overcoat, my walking-stick, my
    gloves
(Which feats of ingenuity his tender mother loves).
He has too little work to do, and much—*too* much
    —of play :
I know a first-rate boarding school a hundred miles
    away.

Suppose upon my lowly suit the wealthy widow
    smiled,
I might assert my claim, perhaps, to castigate the
    child.
No doubt the duty would be mine to exercise a right
Of second-hand paternity upon that widow's mite.

It nearly makes me ill to see a fellow-creature
    weep ;—
Still, boys are very obstinate—and canes are very
    cheap.
'Twould be a sore necessity—but, reader, *entre nous*,
I think that little imp would prove the sorer of the
    two.

I have a turn for wedded life, and long to settle down :
She owns a house in Devonshire—another one in
    town.
I shan't regret the City much : its drudgery I hate :
'Tis only cynics, after all, who scoff at silver plate.
And yet there is a bitter pill, one thorn among the
    flow'rs ;
A nightmare of a deadly form to mock my married
    hours.
The Hymeneal bond, methinks, would bring me little
    joy :
I *might* put up with Edith S——; I *cannot* stand the
    boy !

MY PECULIARITY.

WE poets, when suddenly summoned away
  From the world's petty sphere to the region
   of rhyme,
 The importunate call at a moment obey,
To indulge in the playful or grasp the sublime.
I've indited impromptus again and again,
 While bewildered—it matters not how or by whom ;
I can write at my club, on the boat, in a train ;—
 But I never can write with a wasp in the room.

'Tis twilight. The suburbs are tranquil and calm
 (And my own is as tranquil and calm as the rest);
So I sit by my lattice, inhaling the balm
 That is borne on the zephyr—methinks from the
  west.
I am far from the haunts and the passions of men,
 Among birds in full feather and roses in bloom ;—
What an idyll to-night could I give to my pen !
 But I never could write with a wasp in the room.

From Flora's dominion, ah ! why should he roam,
 To invade—and unbidden—Apollo's domain ?

I opine that his object in tracking me home
    Is to drive the gay anapæsts out of my brain.
Fly away, pretty guest, fly away from the shade !
    'Tis philosophers only that bask in the gloom.
I have money to earn, there is verse to be made ;
    And I never can write with a wasp in the room.

Not gone ?   Very well, then ; 'tis war to the knife.
    I appeal to the *ultima ratio* of kings.
I have proffered you liberty.   Look to your life !
    Cotton handkerchiefs knotted are dangerous things.
If that weapon should fail, there are others in store :
    I've a poker, a shovel, some tongs, and a broom.
I am eager for work, as I told you before ;
    And I never can write with a wasp in the room.

'Tis finished : retributive justice is dealt !
    You may think me severe, but it's one of my ways ;
For, when once an antipathy comes to be felt,
    It is felt evermore to the end of our days.
When my own shall be ended—it matters not how—
    They may carve on the marble that graces my tomb—
" He was not a bad poet, as poets go *now ;*
    But he never could write with a wasp in the room ! "

THE CONTENTED COCKNEY.

LET the cedars of Lebanon squander their shade
 On the Palestine youth or the Palestine
 maid.
To the rose that is queen of thy valley, Cashmere,
Let the nightingale sing what the rose cannot hear.
I suppose that the rose and the cedar must be
Some particular plant and particular tree ;
But they carry no sentiments, tender or grand,
To the soul of a gentleman born in the Strand.

There is grandeur in plenty to capture the eye
Where the proud Himalayas mount up to the sky.
There is food for the fancy as well as the sight
Where the broad Mississippi careers in its might.
But thy mountain, O Ludgate, though scarcely
 sublime,
Hath a charm of its own, and is easy to climb ;
And the best river scenery waits my command
In a glance at the Thames from a street in the
 Strand.

On the peaks of the Tyrol the hunter is heard
As he mocks with his jodel the cloud-loving bird;
And the peasants in France and the gipsies of Spain
Daily carol or dance to some pastoral strain.
Let the gipsies of Spain and the peasants in France
Go ahead—but I neither can carol nor dance;
So I listen, contented and calm, to a band
Of the tuneful Teutonics who favour the Strand.

Let the mountain and river, the cedar and rose,
To the optics of others their beauty disclose.
Let the gipsies and peasants and gay Tyrolese
Grow as fond of their dance and their song as they
        please.
But the soul of the bard, though to limits confined,
Is at least sympathetic and yearns for its kind.
There are themes to infinity always on hand
For the pen of the poet who chants of the Strand.

CUPID'S A B C.

YEARS have elapsed—a few bright, many
    shady—
    (More than I'm willing to say)
Since I devotedly loved a young lady
    Living just over the way.
Sweet seventeen, and as fair as a lily
    (Show me the lily so fair)!
What was the wonder I fell willy-nilly
    Head over heels in the snare?

Only a clerk, not a year from a school yet,
    Wages and wits on a par;
Playing the Romeo to *Somebody's* Juliet,
    Like a true tragedy star.
How could I settle to commerce or trading,
    Toss'd on an ocean of care?
Freighted with doubts (as *per* Love's bill of lading)
    Bound for the Gulf of Despair!

How did I waste the whole mornings together,
　　How by my window I stood,
Waiting and waiting, and wondering whether .
　　Waiting would bring any good.
Smiles and salutes inexpressibly tender
　　Daily went over the street.
I at discretion had made my surrender;
　　Why was not *she* as discreet?

Thanks, many thanks, for thy welcome invention,
　　Friend of the deaf and the dumb;
Lending an ear to the quick apprehension,
　　Speech to the fingers and thumb.
Dear little word!—what a joy to repeat it!
　　First came an L, then an O;
Only two letters it lacks to complete it.
　　Can you imagine them?—No?

Love, beyond pantomime billing and cooing,
　　Made very little advance;
Time, the old meddler, is always undoing
　　All that is done by Romance.
Now that the spell has been long ago broken,
　　Love deaf and dumb I deride:
Now I believe that, if Romeo had *spoken*,
　　Juliet would not have replied.

MY THREE LOVES.

WHEN Life was all a summer day,
    And I was under twenty,
      Three loves were scattered in my way—
   And three at once are plenty.
Three hearts, if offered with a grace,
   One thinks not of refusing.
My task in this especial case
   Was only that of choosing.
        I knew not which to make my pet—
      My pipe, cigar, or cigarette.

To cheer my night or glad my day
   My pipe was ever willing ;
The meerschaum or the lowly clay
   Alike repaid the filling.
Grown men delight in blowing clouds,
   As boys in blowing bubbles ;
Our cares to puff away in crowds,
   And banish all our troubles.
        My pipe I nearly made my pet,
      Above cigar or cigarette.

A tiny paper, tightly rolled
  About some Latakia,
Contains within its magic fold
  A mighty *panacea.*
Some thought of sorrow or of strife
  At ev'ry whiff will vanish ;
And all the scenery of life
  Turn picturesquely Spanish.
        But still I could not quite forget
        Cigar and pipe for cigarette.

To yield an after-dinner puff,
  O'er *demi-tasse* and brandy,
No cigarettes are strong enough ;
  No pipes are ever handy.
However grand may be the feed,
  It only moves my laughter,
Unless a dry delicious weed
  Appears a little after.
        A prime cigar I firmly set
        Above a pipe or cigarette.

But, after all, I try in vain
  To fetter my opinion ;
Since each upon my giddy brain
  Has boasted a dominion.
Comparisons I'll not provoke,
  Lest *all* should be offended.

Let this discussion end in smoke,
   As many more have ended.
      And each I'll make a special pet ;—
      My pipe, cigar, and cigarette.

"TIME! TIME!"

A WEARY, dreary lot is mine—a weary, dreary
life.—
   I wage against my destiny a long and bitter
      strife.
By day and night (though vainly quite) the contest I
   renew.—
Ah, me! that I was ever born a clock of ormolu!
Before a lordly looking-glass, above a pleasant fire,
I ply my task. "What more," you ask, "would any
   clock desire?"—
Away, away! No flesh and blood can properly divine
This tedious, dull monotony that seems for ever mine.

When I was young and innocent I fancied it sublime
To mark each flying footstep of that grand old runner,
   Time.
Like any proper boy or girl who learns the letters
   through,
I did my duty gallantly—for just a year or two.
It seems to me a century! We clocks grow very
   fast.
My baby days are over, and my boyish ones are past.

As model of propriety I've acted pretty long;
But now, I own, I *should* so like—to go a little wrong!

Oh, if my key were only lost, and I could have my
way!—
I'd never be correct again throughout the merry day.
Like any decent horologe I'd never deign to go,
But always be a little fast or else a little slow.
And I would play old gooseberry with men I didn't
like;
And, when it was no hour at all, I'd always give a
strike.
When anybody put me right, I'd get so wrong again,
That nobody should ever be in time for any train.

My master is a flighty wag—well known about the
town;
He treats me very kindly, but resents my running-
down.
And, while he winds me up again, I murmur with a
groan :
" You're fond enough of rest yourself. *Do* leave your
clock alone ! "
He studies metaphysics, and occasionally sends
Nocturnal invitations to his philosophic friends.
I listen while they try to prove the Freedom of the
Will;
Yet, though I strive, I can't contrive to keep one
second still.

B

I've known such gay and giddy clocks—I recollect
   them now—

Brimful of mirth and merriment, they went on *anyhow ;*

As though it mattered not a jot how ill a clock
   behaves,

So long as it can only quote that "Time was made
   for slaves !"

I envy them their liberty ; I pine beneath my chains.

The true Bohemian devilry is running through my
   veins.

Oh, for a single wicked hour !—Pray grant me, Fate,
   the boon

Of striking *one* while yonder sun proclaims the hour
   of *noon !*

AFTER THE BANQUET.

HE revels are over—the orgy is past;
　　All my lively companions have left me at
　　　last;
And the half-dozen strokes of my long-cherished clock
Are effaced by the strains of the shrill-crowing cock.
In its grave lies the laughter that burst from our lips
Over Honeyman's ditties and Funnyman's quips.
Not an echo survives in the dawn's chilly light
Of the mirth and the music that gleamed through the
　　night.

There were dainties of every conceivable shape;
There was Bass—there was Allsopp—and blood of
　　the grape.
There were spirits, arranged by some cunning device
To be not very noxious and yet very nice.
But the thoughts of the feast bring a gloom to my brow,
As I gaze on the wrecks that remain of it *now*;
And a few bitter sentiments enter my head,
While I swiftly but sadly prepare me for bed.

As I glance at yon blank and untenanted shell
Where it once was the pride of an oyster to dwell,
I can scarcely restrain the too sensitive tear
And the wish to behold its inhabitant here.
Yonder bowl, I remember, held salad inside,
Where the herbs and the lobster in interest vied ;
Yonder bottles, once brimming, look now so forlorn
That I trace through their bodies the advent of morn.

Yet why should I murmur?—That sunny Champagne
Was productive of Jones's most rollicking vein ;
And I never believed that young Simmons could pun
Till the serious drink of the night was begun.
Though the scent of tobacco still sickens the air,
My cigars were pronounced a success—and they *were.*
Sammy Travers, who came to me down in the dumps,
Made a joke after three of them.   There are the
     stumps.

Ah, Youth is the gaslight, and Age is the gray,—
Will the follies of night bear the beams of the day ?
It is hardly for butterfly-poets to preach,
But at forty the learner may set up to teach.
Giddy boys go along, with your jokes and your song :
Which are all very pleasant, and not very wrong.
But the dawning of Reason, Philosophy tells,
Only leave empty bottles—and ashes—and shells.

LINES

WRITTEN ON A BANK HOLIDAY.

AURORA brings a sunny day—
    Serene the sky, the air delicious ;
    And lads and lassies all are gay
To find the weather so auspicious.
    In ecstasy without alloy
They chirp the matutinal ditty ;
    And all are yielded up to joy
Who populate our giant city.

Nay, said I "all"? The giddy throng
    May taste the thrill of promised pleasure ;
But not for *me* the frolic song,
    The merry laugh, the mazy measure.
Not mine to join some jolly band,
    But mine to pine in lonely sorrow ;—
The shops are closed along the Strand,
    And closed will be until to-morrow.

Not mine to-day as oftentimes—
    Lulled sweetly by the flowing traffic—

To meditate my modest rhymes,
   The Anapæstic or the Sapphic :
To saunter through the trim Arcade,
   Where toys from ev'ry earthly nation,
With prodigality displayed,
   Entrance the coming generation.

The country always hath a charm
   (Though in my funny moods I quiz it) ;
There scarcely can be any harm
   In paying out-of-town a visit.
But strew your Cockney crowds about—
   Your Jacks, your Jennys, Toms, and Sallys—
They put the tone of landscape out,
   And hardly fit the hills and valleys.

I will not wander miles away,
   To find at ev'ry step a neighbour
Whom in my stroll of ev'ry day
   I meet with at his daily labour.
'Twould be a boon to have him *here*,
   Though I should shun him at a distance ;
My afternoon will all be drear—
   And all for want of his assistance.

A TOWN PASTORAL.

MY Phyllis, of course you remember the day
    When yourself and your Strephon together
Went forth in our childishly innocent way
    For a stroll in the sweet sunny weather.
Of course you remember (or can, if you try)
  That our names were *not* Strephon and Phyllis.
Quite otherwise ;—mine was Ezekiel A. Guy,
  While your own, dear, was Emma J. Willis.

We gazed with a loving but awe-stricken glance
  On the beauty that Nature discloses :
We roamed the *parterre*, and our languid advance
  Was encumbered by lilies and roses.
With buds and with roots, and with blossoms and
    shoots,
  Covent Garden's an Eden to enter ;—
What lips never moistened o'er Solomon's fruits
  In that avenue christened " The Centre " ?

Descending a hillock we came to the stream
  And embarked on a fast-flying shallop ;

Thén, swift as an image that floats through a dream,
  We were borne o'er the waves at a gallop.
I made the remark that in Battersea Park
  There are corners to bill or to coo in ;—
While steamers ply hither and thither till dark,
  And the fares are not absolute ruin.

We dallied with Nature the whole merry day,
  For the whole merry day she enthralled us :
The glow of the Occident faded in gray—
  And then Art in her majesty called us.
Fair Nature awhile has the earth for domain,
  But the accents of Art can we smother ?—
We sat through the whole of *Macbeth* at the "Lane,"
  And admired Barry Something-or-Other.

So spent we in pastoral pleasures each hour—
  (I except the enchantments of Drury !)—
And though *Rus in urbe* was out of our pow'r,
  We transported our *Urbs* into *rure.*
Thus, thus will our days in the future go by ;
  For, if Strephon be dear to his Phyllis,
As true as his name is Ezekiel A. Guy,
  Hers will cease to be Emma J. Willis.

A STUDY ON PHYSICS.

LITTLE Bobby was bright, little Bobby was good ;
    Little Bobby did all that a little boy should ;
    Caring more for his lessons and less for his
        play
Than is common with most little boys of the day.
But, if health be a blessing and sickness a curse,
Little Bobby's position could hardly be worse ;
For a series of maladies (ending in fits)
Shook the system of poor little Bobby to bits.

All the softness and sympathy Nature implants
In the bosoms of parents and uncles and aunts,
On the patient were lavish'd again and again,
And the shops of the chemists were emptied in vain ;
But no powder, no plaister, no potion he tried,
Had the merit of making him better inside.
So the only resource that was left for him still
Was to trust in that horror of horrors—a pill.

Little Bobby was brave, but he shudder'd with dread
From the soles of his boots to the crown of his head

For the terrible truth may as well be unveil'd—
He had lately attempted a pill—but had fail'd !
Oh, the gasp and the gurgle came back to him now,
And the thoughts of the struggle brought beads to his
     brow.
But the doctor was firm.   " Little Bobby," said he,
" 'Tis as easy, my child, as to swallow a pea."

What a hint !—Little Bobby rush'd out for a walk :
To the garden he flew—took a pod from the stalk.
There were six lovely marrowfats, not very small ;
But the boy was a hero—he bolted them all.
For he thought, by beginning to practise on these,
To ingurgitate pills with comparative ease.
So he swallow'd and swallow'd ; in fact, such a lot
That the pods of the marrowfats covered the spot.

But there chanced a mishap for which nobody look'd :
It is rarely that peas will digest when uncook'd.
Little Bobby was taken so frightfully ill
That no physic would cure him, not even a pill.
When they brought him a box with a couple inside,
He disposed of the pair, mutter'd " Thank you "—and
     died ;
And the loss which his parents were left to deplore
Gave to Physical Science one martyr the more.

THE BELLS OF SAINT MARTIN'S.

(WRITTEN IN SICKNESS.)

LYING as close a captive here
    As Damiens on his bed of steel,
    Restless I turn and lend an ear
      To ev'ry fast-revolving wheel.
My spirit would be all unmann'd
    In silent or suburban gloom ;—
But in the gay and giddy Strand
    My Cockney soul hath elbow-room.

I cannot walk ; I cannot stir—
    Save painfully from side to side.
My fate, should any fire occur,
    Simply consists in getting fried.
I dream by day, and watch by night
    The dancing shadows on the wall.
My couch, though not an Eden quite,
    Is not unpleasant, after all.

On Friday nights at eight o'clock
    Begins my merriest of times :

My cradled slumberings to rock
   Ring out Saint Martin's merry chimes.
My head may throb, my bones may ache :
   But—when those happy bells begin—
I murmur (only half awake),
   " Peace to the soul of Nelly Gwynne ! "

The ringers there, across the way,
   Who bid the cheering metal speak,
Receive, as portion of their pay,
   A leg of mutton once a week.
Poor Mistress Eleanor, good soul,
   Bequeathed this banquet in her will.
(Although a sinner on the whole,
   With all her faults I love her still.)

I greet with joy (as many must)
   The merry, merry bells of Yule ;
And never was averse, I trust,
   From any others as a rule.
But none will ever match the mirth
   My favoured belfry's clangour yields.
Of all the chimes on all the earth
   Give *me* Saint Martin's in the Fields !

DIVIDED LOVE.

YOU fear this fickle heart of mine,
  Divided in its duty,
May worship at another shrine
  Before another beauty.
You thought, as many more may do,
  This heart was all your own, dear :
I still declare it beats for you—
  Though not for you alone, dear.

Our loves, when life is young and green,
  Are very true and tender ;
The gushing heart of seventeen
  Is eager to surrender.
But years, alas !—and not a few—
  Since first we met, are flown, dear :
I still am fond enough of you—
  Though not of you alone, dear.

My later letters lack, you say,
  The fervour of my former ;
'Tis useless on a wintry day
  To wish the day were warmer.

My rare epistles, it is true,
    Have lost their summer tone, dear;
But still I correspond with you—
    Though not with you alone, dear.

I scarcely dread another dart
    From Cupid's cruel quiver;
Attacks are scarce upon my heart,
    Though frequent on my liver.
The locks that once were black in hue
    More silvery have grown, dear:
I still am constant, though, to you—
    Though not to you alone, dear.

ON PASTORAL POETRY.

WHAT bores are the bards who endeavour to
   gull us
 By aping the airs of that classical age
When Virgil and Ovid and flowing Catullus
 Described the delights of the plains by the page.
These isles for a century nearly were flooded
 With pastoral poesy, honeyed but slow ;
And, reader, your grandmamma probably studied
 The lyrics of Shenstone and Beattie and Co.

The bard is a "shepherd," and pines to discover
 Where sweet Amaryllis is "tending her flocks ;"
Meantime, as a rule, the disconsolate lover
 His trouble confides to the valleys and rocks.
The pipe that he carries to solace his roaming,
 For melody—not for tobacco—is meant ;
And all the day long, from the dawn to the "gloaming,"
 It worries the echoes to any extent.

Such language is worse than affected or shady ;—
 I never, I own, could exactly explain

Why a modern fine gentleman courting a lady
   Should call her a " nymph " or himself be a " swain."
Suppose it a sin—as it *is*—to play frolics
   In prose or in verse with our dear mother-tongue—
The bards who committed those wicked bucolics
   Are simply the biggest of sinners unhung.

The vapid conceits of their cooing and billing
   Are elegant, maybe, if not very deep ;—
Still, reader, I'm willing to bet you a shilling
   'Twas chiefly as chops that they cared for their sheep.
Their manners are less of the fields than the cities,
   Their loves have a strong metropolitan taint ;
And Nature, as found in their pastoral ditties,
   Is Nature in patches and powder and paint.

THE BARD'S LEGACY.

WHEN I've indited the last of my oddities,
　　Bidding adieu to the children of men;
　Somebody searching amongst my com-
　　　modities
Haply may find this identical pen.
Send it, oh, stranger, to Browning or Tennyson—
　Also the wish that I breathed as my last;—
Bid him accept it, and with it my benison;
　So let its future atone for its past.

Take, too, the pipe that I painted in Maryland;
　Foe of my morning and friend of my night;
Feeding my fancy on Fame and on Fairyland,
　Lulling my brains in its cloudy delight.
Germany owns, in her great universities,
　Sons of tobacco more worthy than I;
Scores who can tell what a blessing and curse it is.—
　Mine shall be Germany's pipe when I die.

C

Close to my heart, 'midst your other discoveries
    Stranger, you'll meet with a ringlet of gold.
(Pardon the weakness ; you know that a lover is
    Mad when he's youthful and worse when he's old.)
If the first owner seemed loth to abandon it,
    More so the present possessor would be.
Stranger, take warning, and lay not a hand on it,
    Even when Death lays a hand upon *me.*

LIFE'S PLAYTHINGS.

AT the age of only eight, you'll forgive me if I
     state
    That there never was a child like *me*:
I was not a bit inclined to devote my little mind
    To the study of my A B C.
I could linger with delight over marbles or a kite,
    And I left it for the humdrum boys
To be fagging all the day, for I fancied when at play
    There was nothing in the world like Toys!

But my heart was in a flame, I remember, when I came
    To the period of soft sixteen:
She was young and very fair, in a frock and curly hair,
    And the colour of her eyes light green.
When I met her (at a dance) how she thrilled me
      with a glance
    And a pressure of her white kid glove:
In a second I was caught, and in ecstasy I thought
    There was nothing in the world like Love!

Then Ambition had a turn, and I felt my bosom burn
    To be ranked among the earth's great men :
So I wrote a little rhyme—just a step from the
       sublime—
    Tho' I reckoned it sublime *just then.*
Quite a year I threw away on a novel and a play,
    That were worthy of a deathless name ;
I was probably deceived, but I verily believed
    There was nothing in the world like Fame !

I was awfully perplext how to fix upon the next
    'Mid the treasures that the earth might hold :
Some were dearer than the rest, but the dearest and
       the best
    And the brightest of them all seemed Gold.
But it may be—after all—even toys begin to pall,
    In the worry of this long, long strife :
All my gods are overthrown, save the last—for I will
       own
    There is nothing in the world like Life !

THE SHORTEST WAY HOME.

I.

"THE shortest way by half a mile—
    I come so very often by it—
    Is up the road, across the stile,
And through the meadow.   Shall we try it?"
    The days were not without a charm
When, talking soft and looking silly,
    My Love and I walked arm-in-arm
Where lanes were lone and fields were stilly.

II.

We found so many things to say
    That always, in the shiny weather,
We took the—well, the *shorter* way,
    To be a longer time together.
We spoke about—(but goodness knows
    Our topics of confabulation)—
About the weather, I suppose,
    The crops, the harvest, and the nation.

III.

At all events, although the talk
    Was rarely wise and never witty,
We ended each successive walk
    With " Home already :—what a pity !"
We might have lost a little ground,
    Through coming by the road selected ;
Yet both agreed that we had found
    The journey shorter than expected.

IV.

Does Life's experiment support
    The paradox that Love proposes ?
Does *any* path seem very short,
    Unless it be a path of roses ?
We seldom find the nearer way ;
    And, if we hit upon and take it,
By creeping on from day to day,
    It seems as long as length can make it.

V.

The way to Fame is never brief,
    The way to Wealth is ever dreary ;
All earthly roads, in my belief,
    Are very long and very weary.
Nay—*one* that leads through care and strife
    Is rapid, when we once begin it :
We take the "short cut" *out* of life,
    Although we take the longest *in* it.

MY ONLY WEAKNESS.

I HAD lately emerged from a charity school,
    And was thought an intelligent boy ;
    I was one of the class that is known as a rule
    By the title of " Hobbledy-hoy."
If you've any conception what sentiment means,
  You can credit my tale when I say
That I fell into love in the course of my teens
  With a nymph living over the way.

I was merely a scrub in an office, E.C.—
    Where I earned my ten shillings a week—
But I felt I could climb to the top of the tree
    By my talents and plenty of " cheek."
Still for good or for evil I courted my fair,
  Though her prospects were not very grand ;
She was one of the chorus at——Never-mind-where—
  Not a million of miles from the Strand.

What a darling it was !—I escorted her back
    From the Temple of Thespis at night.
Though my present was looking remarkably black,
    I'd a future uncommonly bright.
From a boy in the office I grew to be clerk,
    At a figure of sixty *per ann.*
While my love (in low comedy) made such a mark
    That she won all the press to a man.

I was most energetic, and stuck to my desk
    From a quarter to ten until five ;—
While the hope of my future became in burlesque
    The most promising actress alive.
Whether Byron or Albery, Reece or Burnand
    Were the author, I cared not a bit.
In that house, not a million of miles from the Strand,
    My adored was the pet of the pit.

I'm a partner (a junior) in Something and Co. ;
    And am very well off in my way.
To the circle or stalls of an evening I go
    If my lady-love happens to play.
I am elderly now, and—for want of a wife—
    I shall die an old bachelor yet;
But the one little weakness I've known in my life
    I shall never—no, never—forget.

STANZAS.

(BY HAYNES BAYLY THE SECOND.)

THE Broadwood is opened, its tapers are lit,
　　And my hostess implores me to play ;
　She would hear me accompany lines full of
　　　　wit
　In my truly musicianlike way.
But my lyrics were made for the careless and free,
　　When my heart and my spirits were light :
Seek the lays of the lively from others, not *me ;*
　　Let my song be a sad one to-night.

Leave, leave me, fair lady, to chérish my gloom
　　In a corner far, far from the throng :
Let me carry some chair to the end of the room,
　　And retreat from the dance and the song.
Let me mask my depression and veil my despair
　　From the crowd of the brilliant and bright ;
Or, in case you *insist* upon hearing an air,
　　Let my song be a sad one to-night.

I could warble " The Last Rose of Summer," perhaps,
    In a plaintive and exquisite style:
But I know I should simply and feebly collapse
    In my efforts to conjure a smile.
The low-comedy manner, the sickly grimace,
    Would be rather too painful a sight :—
With a load on my bosom, a cloud on my face,
    Let my song be a sad one to-night.

Not a particle, thank you.   No fluids can cheer
    Such a state of dejection as mine.
It resists the seductive advances of beer,
    And refuses the solace of wine.
No, I cannot be comic, fair lady.   I trust
    You regard my refusal aright.
Well, of course, if you *must* have a ballad, you *must*,—
    Let my song be a sad one to-night.

MORE STANZAS.

(BY HAYNES BAYLY THE SECOND.)

I HAVE taken six glasses of sherry,
  I trust they will ask me to sing ;
I am feeling uncommonly merry,
  And pine to go in for my fling.
I would give them no die-away ditty ;
  My lay should be jocund and light.
Bother sentiment—let me be witty ;
  Oh ! let me be comic to-night.

As I sit here alone in a corner—
  A slighted though eminent guest—
I resemble poor little Jack Horner,
  Except that the pie is *non est.*
Yet I fain would be awfully jolly,
  I fain would be gay if I might ;
I am ready for frolic and folly—
  Oh ! let me be comic to-night.

I was grieved when my opulent uncle
  Was taken so terribly ill.
'Tis a fearful affair, a carbuncle ;
  And baffles all medical skill.
He is gone and has left me to suffer :
  But Time puts our sorrows to flight.
He has left me his money, poor buffer :—
  Oh ! let me be comic to-night.

Let me try ; I am perfectly ready,
  I've sat in this corner too long ;
But my legs are a little unsteady—
  That wine was remarkably strong.
Did you say I was tipsy ? Oh gammon !
  Just lift me up gently. All right.—
I can sing, sir. 'Twas only the salmon.
  Oh ! let me be comic to-night.

OLD CLOTHES.

I'VE a mortal abhorrence, I vow and protest,
    For a coat—or for trousers—that pass for my
        " best ; "
    And a deed I abominate having to do
Is to shine in a waistcoat aggressively new.
Could a Lincoln and Bennett be mine as a gift—
(Not the spoil of my talents or price of my thrift),
I would sneak through the suburbs at night with it on,
Till its gloss were departed—its freshness were gone.

But, alas, for the pride of the children of men !
E'en the cynic invests in a suit now and then ;
Though he basks in the torrent and welcomes the
    storm,
As he waits for the ravages Time will perform :
And he chuckles for glee when his garb he can see
Growing threadbare at elbow and polished at knee ;
Till the symptoms of age crowd around it at last,
And its bloom and its brightness are dreams of the
    past.

Then a day shall be born when but Chaos remains
Of that faithful companion in pleasures and pains—
When the button shall droop like the rose on her stem,
And the fissures gape frequent and wide in the hem;—
When the rents and the patches their presence proclaim
In the boldness of pride that is offspring of shame ;—
And the wearer can deem it not cruel nor strange
That the voice of Society clamours for Change.

While he ferrets his bygone habiliments out,
He exults in the joys of the huntsman or scout ;
Not a nook—not a corner—but straightway unfolds
A Potosi complete in the treasures it holds.
Not a coat—not a waistcoat or trouser—but shows
A regenerate novelty born of repose ;
And the suits that were banished as faded and worn
Look as fresh as the dewdrop that gleams in the morn.

And moreover, whilst looking o'er garments of old
('Tis a fact that my reader may like to be told),
You have pleasant surprises again and again ;
For you rarely can guess what the pockets contain.
Let me tell you a thing that occurred to myself
With some raiment I'd long ago laid on the shelf ;—
While exploring in quite a promiscuous way
I discovered the change for a shilling one day !

MY CONTINENTAL TOUR.

AT eight exactly I awoke—
    At nine had breakfast in a hurry ;
Then o'er my matutinal smoke
    Devoted half an hour to " Murray."
For, weary of the tedious town,
    I longed to leave its commonplaces ;
To search all Europe up and down
    For novel scenes and novel faces.

I fancied I should like the North,
    Especially the coast of Sweden ;
Yet southern climes are imaged forth
    In " Murray " as a kind of Eden.
'Twas ten o'clock, and still I sat
    Without a definite suggestion.
I thought of this and thought of that ;
    But thought of nothing to the question.

Eleven struck.   My feeble mind
  No settled resolution guided.
The noonday only came to find
  My plan of action undecided.
I read the "Telegraph," the "Times,"
  The "Standard," and the "Advertiser."
'Twas one by old St. Clement's chimes,
  And I was not a whit the wiser.

I thought of roving up the Rhine,
  But steamers are my heart's abhorrence.
Another little scheme of mine
  Was traversing the Alps to Florence.
Till two o'clock I strove to make
  My plans, but got uncertain—very ;
And so I sallied forth to take
  A sandwich and a glass of sherry.

From three to four and four to five
  My thoughts were in a dire confusion,
And would not aid me to arrive
  At any definite conclusion.
At six I hurried off to dine,
  Smoked three Manillas *con amore,*
And reached the opera by nine
  To hear a little *Trovatore.*

'Tis twelve o'clock.   I've been to sup.
   This melancholy day is ended.
I rather think of giving up
   The little trip that I intended.
The hours will soon be growing small ;
   I can't sit up another minute :
I won't go out of town at all,
   But pass July and August *in* it.

THE LANGUAGE OF LOVE.

ALK to me only with thine eyes,
  And I will hear with mine ;
  Turn hither all the light that lies
  In those twin orbs of thine.
I shall not miss an H or two,
  Nor find as many slips
Of grammar as I daily do
  From those bewitching lips.

In such a deep impassioned glance,
  Could any eye suspect
A double negative, perchance ;—
  Which never ain't correct.
Could any dazzled gaze descry,
  In stars thus blue and bright,
A tendency to say, "Says I ;"—
  Which, I says, can't be right.

Nay, Love and Prosody combined
  Sit smiling evermore
Within those eyes that speak a mind
  Above grammatic lore.
Those lips may err—they often do ;
  But why should that surprise?
My love has nothing of the Blue
  About her but her eyes.

MISS ASTERISK.

(A DRAMATIC BIOGRAPHY.)

THIS lucky day I mean to lay before my lucky
  reader
    A memorial of the trials and the triumphs of
    a "star."
Thalia, 'midst your followers we rarely find a leader;
  And how very few the leaders who can lead us
    very far;
The naughty time, the merry time, has flown away for
  ever,
    When the lords adored a Woffington, the wits a
    Kitty Clive.
Our comedies were wicked, still our comedies were
  clever,
    While our Kitty was amongst us and our Woffington
    alive.

Miss A. adorned a pantomime, a long-ago December,
   In a far-away locality but little known to Fame.
How deeply she delighted me I vividly remember,
   And I fondly fancied Asterisk an angel of a name.
She spoke—'twas but a word or two.   The part was
     not a long one.—
   How I drank the modulations of her ev'ry gushing
     tone !
(My rapturous impression may, of course, have been
     a wrong one ;
   And I scarcely need inform you that her name was
     not her own.)

Provincial pits and galleries were not for such a
     creature,
   With a face and with a figure for the boxes and the
     stalls.
She invaded our metropolis, and shortly was a feature
   As a photo at the stationer's—a poster on the
     walls.
The character she opened in' evades my recollec-
     tion,
   Though I seem, as in a vision, to behold her in it
     yet.
(And yet I seem to fancy, on deliberate reflection,
   She personified a chambermaid—or, *Gallicè*, sou-
     brette.)

We lost her. She deserted us, to traverse the Atlantic;
  And she now enthralls Americans in farces or bur
    lesque.
She left our country suddenly, and sent me semi-
    frantic ;
  For the comedy I wrote for her is rotting in my desk.
I strive to track her whereabouts—to trumpet her
    successes ;
  But, alas ! my hopes diminish to a tiny little gleam.
Fate limits my discoveries to tiny little guesses,
  And the mem'ry of Miss Asterisk is nothing but a
    dream.

MEDITATIONS.

(BY A LOWTHER ARCADIAN.)

HALL I seek out a gift for my fair—
    For a damsel of sweet seventeen,
    With a forest of gold-coloured hair,
And the bluest of eyes ever seen ?
From the ardent assaults of the sun
    I retreat for a while to the shade ;
Cannot *some* little traffic be done
    While I lounge through the Lowther Arcade ?

What a galaxy beams on my sight
    As I blithely but leisurely roam !
What a chance for conferring delight
    On a too-thickly tenanted home !
Here the grandpapa's heart and his dame's,
    And the hearts of the girls and the boys,
May all proffer their manifold claims,
    From yon spectacles down to yon toys.

Shall I purchase a fife and a drum?
    E'en for babyhood music hath charms.
What a terror such things may become
    In the hands of an infant in arms!
But affrighted humanity shrinks
    From such barbarous weapons in dread;
I will treat her young brother, methinks,
    To a boxful of soldiers instead.

I must think of her sister, of course
    ('Tis a sweet, pretty, innocent thing!);
Shall my choice be a small wooden horse,
    Or a dainty wax doll with a spring?
She will cherish the latter, perhaps,
    And at first be *so* proud of her prize;
But, alas! not a month will elapse
    Ere she pokes out its bright little eyes.

It is time that I thought of my fair
    (As my fair may be thinking of *me*)—
Far from easy the task, I declare,
    To decide what my present shall be.
But, behold, there is sunshine above—
    Let me quit the Arcade for the Strand.
By and by I will call on my love,
    And present her—my heart and my hand.

HISTORIC DOUBTS.

COCKAYNE is deserted and empty to-day,
    For our uncles, our aunts, and our cousins
    Have cut the poor city, and hastened away
    Into parts that are foreign, by dozens.
And there will they listen to legends and lies—
    For each land has its mythical glories—
And open their mouths and their ears and their eyes
    Over tales that are nothing but stories.

Some, bent upon Paris, will cross to Dieppe,
    And may possibly linger at Rouen,
To view the Cathedral—it stands but a step
    From the solemn and stately Saint Ouen.
The crammers in fashion about the Pucelle
    They may treat with derision and laughter ;
If burnt—she got over the accident well,
    For she lived half a century after !

Fair Switzerland, clime of the mountain and lake,
    Hath a charm and a spell for the rover.
Lucerne, for example,—unless we mistake—
    Is a stream that is worth tripping over.
Traditions of Tell and of Gessler are told,
    As a proof how the truth may be twisted ;—
Poor William !   He *would* have been awfully bold
    If poor William had ever existed.

When Brussels he visits, the roamer will find
    That his national pride may be flattered ;
To gaze on that field he of course is inclined
    Where the hopes of Napoleon were shattered.
Of Wellington's fame let the Briton discourse ;
    He believes in it—sings of it—spouts it.
That battle was won, though, by Prussians, of course ;
    And there breathes not a Prussian who doubts it.

The farther we wander, the more we perceive
    (As a fact it is folly denying),
This world from the birthdays of Adam and Eve,
    Has been terribly given to lying.
When incidents happen right under my nose
    I can yield them unlimited credit ;
But, thanks to my training, I'm not one of those
    Who believe in a thing when they've read it.

A WORM IN THE BUD.

'EN as a centipede amongst the roses,
    Concealment fed upon my damask cheek ;
    The secrets that a bolder love discloses
      Mine would have owned, but recked not how
        to speak.
Fain on my knees before my lovely lady
    Could I have cooed like any turtle-dove—
Alack ! my pow'rs of rhetoric were shady,
    So I was coy—I never told my love.

Oft I did marvel whether she suspected
    The hidden pain that wrought my soul's annoy ;
In company methought that she affected
    To treat me as a wild and wayward boy.
Once and again in charity she gave me
    A tress of hair, a photograph, a glove.
Thus, link by link, the more did she enslave me ;
    But I was mute—I never told my love.

We both were poor—not indigent precisely,
  But far from opulent or well to do.
I had been educated rather nicely,
  And oft by verse could earn a pound or two ;
My dear one made a trifle by tuition,
  But had no expectations from her " guv. ; "
Small chance was there to better our condition,
  So I was dumb—I never told my love.

This agony, that made me daily thinner,
  At length reduced me to a shocking state ;
I shunned my breakfast, never touched my dinner,
  And left my supper steaming on my plate.
Upon the dizzy brink of desperation
  I tottered, waiting for the final shove ;
And still, with any martyr's resignation,
  I held my tongue—I never told my love.

Meanwhile her uncle (having lost his liver
  In Indian climes, and grown a wealthy man)
Caught cold while fishing in the Hooghly river,
  And straight came back again from Hindostan.
Scarce had he reached our country ere he perished,
  And left his niece an heiress.   Powers above !
Could I conceal the passion I had cherished ?
  Not for a moment—so I told my love !

TOO GOOD FOR HIS PLACE.

(A COVENT GARDEN PASTORAL.)

YOUNG Colin must quit the fair meadows of
　　Kent,
　　On a trip to Great Britain's gay capital bent;
Brief leisure is Colin's of Daphne to dream,
As he pilots his waggon and whips up his team.
For the lord of young Colin hath acres to farm—
'Tis a trade that is not without merit or charm;—
And he makes it his pride, by all possible means,
To supply the big City with carrots and greens.

The team and the waggon progress through the night
(Until eastward are traces of dawn's ruddy light).—
See, they traverse the Thames, and they traverse the
　　Strand,
And the lamps of the Market at last are at hand.
Then Colin repairs to a tavern hard by—
For the journey was lonesome, and Colin is dry.
And he thinks, while he drinks of his—never-mind-
　　what,
O'er the memories dear to that classical spot.

"Ah, shades of the wealthy—the gay—the re-
    nowned—
Yet again do ye hover this precinct around ;
Yet again with emotion your worshipper thrills,
While he watches ye crowding to Button's and Will's.
Our Congreve and Wycherley, Dryden and Pope,
Never more in the flesh to behold can we hope ;
Still their spirits are here, 'mid the mart's busy din,—
Waiter !—Talking of spirits—a little more gin !

" Not a step from the corner was Garrick's abode—
Kitty Clive had a residence over the road ;
Here Churchill has rhymed on his dark second floor,
And the gallants have knocked at Peg Woffington's
    door.
Harry Fielding's papa, the much-dreaded Sir John,
Was the Midas of Bow Street, a little way on.
What ghosts reappear 'mid the mart's busy hum !—
Waiter !—Keep'st thou the fluid called Pine-apple
    rum ?

" Yon churchyard can boast of remarkable bones,
Though yon church be unworthy of Inigo Jones ;
And yon pile at the corner—called Evans's now—
Echoed once the grand accents of Siddons, I trow.
To the deathless departed again let me drink.—
Waiter !—Fill me my goblet once more to the brink.
This libation—the last one—I'll solemnly pour :
Then return to take charge of that waggon and four !"

TRIBULATIONS OF A HAM SANDWICH.

WHEN our lives are in the gloaming, and the
    night comes hither fast,
    Stern Mem'ry beckons back again the sun-
    light of the past.
The task becomes a torture as we sadly reckon o'er
The delights and the ambitions that are flown for
    evermore.
The last of my companions disappeared this very
    morn ;
He has left me to my solitude, neglected and forlorn.
Alas ! my sole employment is to heave the bitter sigh,
And recall my double birthplace in the cornfield and
    the stye.

But away, fond recollections ! A distinguished Poet
    sings
"That a sorrow's crown of sorrow is rememb'ring
    happier things."
Why dwell on reminiscences that summon me so far,
While pining ignominiously within this tavern bar ?

I vainly seek from dawn till eve to tempt the outer
world
With coagulated mustard and a corner crisply curled.
The most untutored epicure would spurn me where I
lie,
And the famine-stricken mendicant would coldly pass
me by.

Can aught retard the wing of Time? Say, visionary
wild,
Canst look to feel in middle age the freshness of the
child?
The cruel hand of Destiny—no failing of my own—
Hath struck me down in sorrow here—stale, crumpled
and alone.
Three days agone, or little more, my brief career
began!
I then was topmost in the crowd, the leader of my
clan.
We braved the rivalry of beef—of buns—of bread and
cheese ;—
We braved, to speak in metaphor, the battle and the
breeze.

That merry time is over : it was yet for me to learn
All the horrors of an atmosphere that made my edges
turn ;—

And the fumes of the tobacco, and the odours of the
drink,
And a hundred other miseries too deep for pen and
ink.
While ghostly waiters flitted on their duty to and fro,
I courted public appetite where lunchers come and go;
But they deemed me all unfitted for their palates or
their teeth,
So they lifted me, and bore away a friend from under-
neath.

And thus my life has crawled along till not a hope
survives
But that of being bolted by the boy who cleans the
knives:
I have my doubts about him—he's a hungry-looking
brat,
But I hardly dare to fancy he would stoop so low as
that !
I might be handed over to the kittens or the pup;
But my mustard is against me—they would cock their
noses up.
I believe, if I were offered them for food this very day,
That the dog would never touch me, while the cats
would run away.

ESSAY ON THE MOTH.

BY A SENTIMENTAL NATURALIST.

OH, the gay giddy moth is a child of the air,
    That exults in the breezes of summer ;
    'Tis just at the season when blossoms are
      fair
That we hail with delight the new-comer.
    Nor daylight alone to the rover is dear ;
For by night—which is rather imprudent—
    It glads him to hover unpleasantly near
To the taper that gleams for the student.

Oh, it is not alone to the sunshine above
    That the wanderer flies for enjoyment ;
No—e'en for the cottage he nurtures a love,
    And the palace may find him employment.
Unheeded and quiet, he likes to repose
    Amid heaps of respectable raiment ;
In solitude eating his way as he goes,
    With immunity as to the payment.

But, alas ! there are beings remorseless enough
    To convey to the place of his dwelling.
Tobacco and lavender, camphor and snuff,
    Which he soon grows aweary of smelling.
Ah, who could proceed in this barbarous way,
    If he felt—as I feel to my sorrow—
How oft the poor victim who revels to-day
    Is unsure of a meal for to-morrow !

I have suffered, how long? from the gay giddy moth,
    And have pined from his ruthless excesses.
A swallow-tailed garment of daintiest cloth
    Is the lightest of all my distresses.
Sad loss !—I would gladly have tried to devote
    All the means in my pow'r to avoid it.—
I weep for my only respectable coat,
    But I trust the poor creature enjoyed it !

"A WOMAN'S THOUGHTS ABOUT WOMEN."

I THINK Miss Juliet in the play
    A forward little minx;
  (And Mrs. Grundy loves to say
    What Mrs. Grundy thinks).
Her goings-on with Montague,
  I think, were quite absurd;
Such brazen conversation, too,
  I think I never heard.

I think Othello much to blame
  For braving married life
With Desdemona What's-her-Name,
  His worse than wicked wife.
To run away at such an age,
  And with a *nigger*, too :—
Such conduct, even on the stage,
  I think I never knew.

I think, respecting Beatrice,
    Her husband was a flat
If he expected any peace
    With such a girl as that.
Her acts were never very strict,
    Her talk was only jaw;
So green a youth as Benedict
    I think I never saw.

I think, when Portia's wooers came
    To play at pitch-and-toss,
The gentleman that won the dame
    Distinctly won a loss.
I think Emilia was a shrew,
    And Rosalind ill-bred ;
(Such words—and from a lady, too—
    I think I never read).

I think Macbeth was led astray
    By naughty Lady M.
And those three witches—by the way,
    I don't think much of *them.*
I think Ophelia—that's a fact—
    The best of all the set ;
But anybody quite so crack'd
    I think I never met.

A VERY OLD FRIEND.

(IN A VERY NEW DRESS).

" How doth the little——"—DOCTOR WATTS.
" Improve each——"—MORAL SONG.

HE blossoms of Hybla, the buds of Hymettus—
    Old Sicily's glory, old Attica's pride ;—
      In dreams we have sipped, long as Fancy
        would let us,
  The nectar those blossoms and buds have supplied.
In dreams we have envied each gay busy rover
  Who stole from the summer the sweets of its prime;
Who left the wild buttercups, daisies, and clover,
  For marjoram's odours and essence of thyme.

At eve, when the wanderer—weary with roaming—
  In laden satiety flew to its nest,
New trials and cares would encumber the gloaming,
  And Hesperus never gave token of rest.
What poet can picture with any precision
  The trials domestic economy breeds,
When Paterfamilias attempts a provision
  For family wishes and family needs ?

The mind philosophic, on energy musing,
   Elects as a model the hive of the bee ;
A home so domestic—if mine were the choosing—
   Would surely be safest and fittest for *me.*
To banish the bowl and the dance and the revel
   Would suit my ambition, I candidly think ;—
To stroll through my life at a sober dead-level,
   And live with my paper, my pens, and my ink.

'Twas thus the grave Stoics and Peripatetics
   Gave each of their minutes to learning alone ;—
They taught metaphysics and studied æsthetics,
   And left us a glory completely their own.
My ink and my paper and pens I will cherish,
   And leave to the world all the wisdom I may ;—
To murmur at last, when I'm ready to perish,
   " *Non perdidi diem*—I've not lost a day ! "

HOW IT OCCURRED.

HE said—But shall my pen betray
   The words I cannot speak ?
  No ; rather let Concealment prey
   Upon my damask cheek.
I feel that Happiness and Mirth
  May come again in glee
To every other soul on earth—
  But not again to *me.*

She said—But wherefore wake again
  The memories of the past ?
Let Life remain a desert-plain,
  And skies be still o'ercast.
She said—But shall I dare to fight
  Against my Fate's decree?
Let Hope to others bring delight—
  She bringeth none to *me.*

I told her—But it matters not ;—
    The past could be effaced,
Were I to find some sunny spot
    In Life's eternal waste.
She answered—But I little care
    How dark my path may be.
Let Peace go smiling ev'rywhere,
    No smile she brings to *me*.

IF!

(AN ALMOST PATRIOTIC SONG.)

IF skies were bluer,
   And fogs were fewer,
     And fewer the storms on land and sea ;—
   Were shiny summers
   Perpetual comers—
What an Utopia this would be !

   If Life were longer,
   And Faith were stronger,
If Pleasure would bide—if Care would flee ;
   If each were brother
   To all the other—
What an Arcadia this would be !

   Were Greed abolished,
   And Gain demolished,
Were slavery chained and Freedom free ;
   If all earth's troubles
   Collapsed like bubbles—
What an Elysium this would be !

"BRAG!"

THE throng unpoetic may cock up their noses,
  And sneer as they list at the triumphs of
    Mind,
But the life of the bard is a pathway of roses ;
  A feast of ambrosia, with nectar combined.
My career was a solitude fit for a hermit
  Till Poesy brought me success and renown ;
And at present—I mildly but proudly affirm it—
  I know all the authors and actors in town.

T'other day—and the day I shall fondly remember—
  I met Mr. Tennyson taking a walk ;
And—a singular fact !—in the month of September,
  I twice overheard Barry Sullivan talk.
Then I *was* to have met Mr. Phelps at a supper,
  But poor Sammy Phelps was unluckily ill ;
And I recently wrote an epistle to Tupper,
  Who sent me no answer—but possibly *will*.

A relation of mine, whom I love pretty dearly,
    Has long been a neighbour of Thomas Carlyle's
For one peep at so deep a philosopher merely
    I'd walk with alacrity two or three miles.
To his trim little garden in moments of leisure
    The Teacher goes frequently forth for a crawl ;
And it's thus I contrive with devotional pleasure
    To gaze upon Thomas from over the wall.

At the Albion I mix with your drinkers and smokers,
    For wags of the maddest are there to be met ;
There are Hollingshead, Byron, and such merry
        jokers,
    And Gilbert, Burnand, and the cream of the set.
Such wit, and such humour ! Say, where can you
        match them ?—
    Their quips and the cranks are the best of the day ;
Only somehow I never can properly catch them,
    From sitting some two or three boxes away.

So I drink to my Muse and my patron Apollo,
    Who taught me to thread the recesses of rhyme ;
For the bard's is a princely profession to follow—
    Parnassus a rosy excrescence to climb.
I see in my visions Calliope flying
    To bear my renown to posterity down ;
I can hear her exalting my merits, and crying—
    " He knew all the authors and actors in town ! "

ALL ABROAD.

I'VE journeyed over many seas,
    And wandered under many skies;
I've hoarded knowledge by degrees,
    Some useful and some otherwise.
My Fatherland I fondly call
    The dearest corner of the earth ;
And yet I scarcely know at all
    The British Isles that gave me birth.

All mountain-peaks to me are fair ;
    I fondly love the lovely Alps ;
What curly clouds they daily wear,
    Like wigs upon their snowy scalps !
O'er all their passes have I been,
    And scaled their very highest height ;
Helvellyn I have never seen,
    While Snowdon is a stranger quite.

Still treasured for their own sweet sakes,
    To memory oft and oft return
Helvetia's clear and placid lakes,
    Geneva—Zurich—and Lucerne.
Italia, too, hath blessed my sight
    With lakes as placid and as clear ;
Yet never did these eyes alight
    On Derwent or on Windermere.

I've watched with awe thine angry strife,
    Sublime Schaffhausen, o'er and o'er.
I never chanced in all my life
    To view thy cataract, Lodore.
With tardy mules and lazy wheels
    The *diligence* has dragged me far ;—
I cannot fancy how it feels
    To traverse Dublin on a car.

My cosmopolitan career
    At last is drawing to a close :
I'll dedicate at least a year
    To things beneath my very nose.
Considering that I stand so high
    As master of so many styles,
I *may* complete before I die
    A " Guide-Book to the British Isles."

MY OLD ARM-CHAIR.

LOATHE it—I loathe it—and who shall dare
   To chide me for loathing my own arm-chair?
   It haunts me daily, and wheels its flight
Into the dreams that I dream by night.
When I look at its cover of outworn chintz,
Where age and washing have blurred the tints,
No earthly passion can well compare
With my deadly hate for that old arm-chair.

I loved with a love of the noblest kind ;—
Sensitive—delicate—most refined.
But she spurned my love and betrayed her vow,
And is only a Mrs. McKenzie now.
I cannot forget though I might forgive ;—
My wrongs will follow me whilst I live.
But *this* is the memory worst to bear ;—
She once took tea in that old arm-chair.

I owned a creditor—(frightful man !)—
Who bored me as creditors only can.
He vaguely talked of a small amount
Which took the shape of an old account.
Twice in the week, I remember well,
He banged my knocker or twanged my bell.
If he found me without any cash to spare,
He called me names from that old arm-chair.

Incubi, demons, nightmares, owls,
Vampires, goblins, ghosts, and ghouls,
Visit that seat, and around it swarm
In every possible shape and form.
My life is a torture, a perfect curse—
My home is a dungeon, or something worse
I shall never be happy or freed from care
Until I get rid of that old arm-chair.

MY FELLOW-TRAVELLER.

I'VE met a million ugly men
 In going east and going west.
I've met, it may be, nine or ten
 More ugly than the ugly rest.
But never gazed I anywhere
 Upon a face—until to-day—
Distinctly qualified to bear
 The palm of ugliness away.
        These lines—my beautiful, my own—
        I write for *you*—and you alone.

At Hammersmith I caught the train,
 And sought my lowly second-class.
All suddenly a window-pane
 Revealed your visage through the glass.
I oped the door—I know not how—
 Perhaps I seemed abruptly rude ;
But inly I had formed a vow
 To come and share your solitude.
        These lines—my beautiful, my own—
        I write for *you*—and you alone.

F

I've read a very ghastly tale
  About a very ghastly man,
Who hid himself within a veil,
  And went about in Khorassan.
He came to grief, unless I err;
  And in a caldron took a dive.
Believe me, I am happy, Sir,
  To find that *you* are still alive.
      These lines—my beautiful, my own—
      I write for *you*—and you alone.

I felt within my bosom rise
  A pleasure not unmixed with awe,
When slumber closed your leaden eyes,
  And sleep unlocked your nether jaw.
I give you, for your own sweet sake,
  This proverb—new, and rather deep;—
True Ugliness, when wide awake,
  Is pale to Ugliness asleep.
      These lines—my beautiful, my own—
      I write for *you*—and you alone.

We flew along from place to place;—
  You never moved, you never woke;
While, gazing on your placid face,
  I smoked a philosophic smoke.

At length we came to Charing Cross ;—
　How brief, alas ! the journey seems.
I left you—and I felt the loss—
　But I regained you in my dreams.
　　　These lines—my beautiful, my own—
　　　I write for *you*—and you alone.

MEDITATIONS ON A FRANKFORT SAUSAGE.

THE more profoundly men reflect,
    The more they find, by Logic's laws,
  That what at first is called *Effect*
    In course of time becometh *Cause.*
Of ev'ry link in Matter's chain
  The end and origin are clear ;
Yet Reason seems to ask in vain,
    " How came the Frankfort sausage here ? "

Behold the meek and lowly hen !—
  The timely egg will she produce.
(That egg, though addled now and then,
  Will now and then be fit for use.)
Observe how Nature hath her ways
  Above the petty ways of men :—
Yon timely egg, ere many days,
  May grow a meek and lowly hen.

Yet no analysis may test—
    Although it strive and strive again—
This gloomy, dark, forbidding guest
    That hails from Frankfort-on-the-Maine.
Of all beside we trace the birth ;
    We know the when—the where—the how.
Oh say, grim sojourner on earth,
    Mysterious Being—what art *thou?*

Did Nassau nurse thy glowing youth
    Amongst the valleys and the rocks?
Wast thou a boar—nay, tell the truth—
    Or part of thee, perchance, an ox?
Thou hadst a mother—hadst thou not?
    No doubt thou also hadst a sire :—
But each, by Fortune's bitter lot,
    Hath passed before thee to the fire.

But wherefore dig thy sorrows up,
    Or broach a theme so full of gloom ?—
Lo, thou hast quaff'd thy bitter cup,
    And mash'd potatoes are thy doom.
It boots not whether beef or pork ;—
    Why risk these wild hypotheses ?—
Go, Mary, bring a knife and fork ;
    And fetch the mustard, if you please !

THE FORSAKEN ONE.

THE dark, chilly nights of the winter are near,
    And the shrill cry of " Muffins" is heard
        in the land ;
As I strive, sitting sadly in solitude here,
    To evoke the gay verse from the frost-bitten hand ;
But I care not—the days may be drear as they will,
    And the flowers may be faded, the birds may be
        flown ;
There is one living creature that clings to me still ;—
    'Tis the last fly of Summer, left brooding alone.

On my half-covered foolscap he crawls to and fro,
    And his wings flip my vowels and consonants by.
It were well that he tarried one minute, or so,
    Till the passionate lines on my paper grew dry.
From a blue-inky grave have I rescued him twice ;
    It is time I asserted a will of my own.
Let me blandly administer words of advice
    To the last fly of Summer, left brooding alone.

" Ah, wherefore, thou lingerer, wherefore delay ?
    All thy lively companions are banished or slain.
Look alive—make an effort—go, haste thee away
    To fair Italy's climate, or sweet sunny Spain.
There are dangers in store—oh, believe in thy bard—
    When the cold bitter blasts of the autumn have
        blown ;
And the winter will turn out uncommonly hard
    For the last fly of Summer, left brooding alone.

" When the Ulster descends from its home on the
        hook,
    And the warmth-giving wrappers return from the
        wash ;—
When the coyly-hid comforter starts from its nook,
    And we hunt up the ugly but useful golosh ;—
When the ornaments glitter no more on the stove,
    And the morn wears a cheerless and menacing
        tone ;—
It will all be intensely unpleasant, by Jove !
    To the last fly of Summer, left brooding alone.

" 'Twill be mercy, perchance, can I spare thee the
        ills
    That arise from the fogs, and the frosts, and the
        snow ;

From the colds, the rheumatics, the coughs, and the
    chills,
    Which envelop mankind from the top to the toe.
It will take but a second—one stroke of my pen ;—
    It will cost thee no pang—not a sigh, not a groan.
Far away will the world and its troubles be *then*
    From the last fly of Summer, left brooding alone.

THE MUSIC OF THE PAST.

ET Wagner—the Bard of the Future—go hang,
    With his rumpus and riot and rattle :—
    His praise may be penn'd by a critical gang,
  But I heed not a tittle their tattle.
No tune of the future or present can yield
  Such a charm to this organ auricular
As yielded the ditties of Dibdin and Shield,
  And of Arne—yes, of Arne in particular.

Old melodies haunt me from long, long ago,
  Of a taste and a style that have perished.
Excuse me,—I'm rather old-fashioned, you know ;
  And I love what my grandmamma cherished.
Though years have escaped me, like so many days,
  The desire is incessantly lingering
To listen once more while my grandmamma plays,
  With her comical *rococo* fingering.

She sang, too—a little—did grandmamma dear ;—
    She would garnish a fugue of Scarlatti,
By letting me hear " Said a Smile to a Tear,"
    Or by crooning my pet *"Batti, batti."*
To grasp at the latter would cost me a strain ;
    For—though always a creature of sentiment—
I caught but a word of it now and again,
    Only knowing what one out of twenty meant.

We fogies have often a way, it appears
    (And a way it is folly concealing),
Of letting our hearts run away with our ears,
    And our science elope with our feeling.
Those tones of the past, that have sunk to their
        tomb,
    May at present be laughed at as funny ones ;—
I cling to them still in the hours of my gloom,
    For they carry me back to my sunny ones.

A PLAIN COOK.

ONE Hannah Glasse, a homely dame,
    Long long ago produced a book
    (For fun—for profit—or for fame)
Which taught our grannies how to cook.
Suppose we run it through, and seize
    A stray quotation as we pass.
To dress a Hare.—Attention, please !—
    " First catch your Hare," says Hannah Glasse.

Methinks 'tis easy, reader dear,
    To find a moral in the phrase.—
I've dreamed about a bright career
    Through half my nights and all my days.
By day and night my visions bring
    A bard's ambition ; but, alas !
My Muse is dumb and cannot sing.—
    " First catch your Hare," says Hannah Glasse.

It is not meet the poet's life
   Should pass untended and alone ;—
I'd fain discover in a wife
   Some heart responsive to my own.
No proud patrician would I woo,
   Nor one of the plebeian class ;
But something just between the two.—
   " First catch your Hare," says Hannah Glasse.

With just a thousand pounds a year,
   Proceeding from the Three-per-cents,
My future might be pretty clear
   (With something in the way of rents).
But gold is not for such as I ;
   My stock in trade is only brass,
I *may* be wealthy by-and-by.—
   " First catch your Hare," says Hannah Glasse.

USED UP.

IN Canada this afternoon
      They chase the grisly bear,
      While swarth Kentucky hunts the coon
  Or seeks the 'possum's lair.
Nor coons nor 'possums *I* pursue,
  Nor court the bear's embrace ;
I can but maim a cat or two—
  My life is commonplace.

The Sallee rover after dark
  Will sweep across the sea ;
The Algerine will steer his bark
  In search of £ *s. d.*
When *I* desire to go afloat
  (Which rarely is the case),
I can but seek the Chelsea boat—
  My life is commonplace.

The roundelay of rapture fills
  The valleys of Cashmere ;
The river dances, and the hills
  Are stooping down to hear.
Of music, frankly I avow,
  I scarcely own a trace ;
I can but make a jolly row—
  My life is commonplace.

Constantinople's minarets
  Gleam brightly in the sun ;
He slowly sets, and half regrets
  His daily work is done.
The view *I* get from my domains
  Is limited in space ;
I can but see Saint Clement Danes—
  My life is commonplace.

In Timbuctoo, a blest retreat,
  Where Instinct stands for Law,
To-night perchance the chiefs will eat
  A missionary raw.
Full gladly *I* would sit and take
  My meals with such a race ;
I can but order chop or steak—
  My life is commonplace.

I hate the rules that bind me down
   Within my native isle ;
I wish to travel out of town,
   And let my domicile.
In short, I wish to overhaul
   The universe's face,
And shift my quarters once for all—
   My life is commonplace.

REAL FRIENDS.

F all the blessings we enjoy—
    Of all the treasures Luck may send—
    For man mature, or growing boy,
  The brightest is a bosom-friend.
True bosom-friends to me have been—
    Though neither of my kin or kith—
My close companions Tommy Green,
    And Freddy Brown, and Sammy Smith.

In Tommy Green's expressive eye
    The passions of the lion shine ;
How like the lightning would he fly
    To crush to dust some foe of mine !
But could I calmly to the fight
    Expose the truest soul alive ?—
I'm half-a-dozen feet in height,
    While Tommy Green is under five.

At any stage of Life's career,
  Should fickle Fortune on me frown,
My ruined state would call the tear
  From sympathetic Freddy Brown.
The world would not be all a blank—
  One solace would remain for me ;—
But I've a balance at my bank,
  While Fred is always "up a tree."

Were I in lack of good advice,
  Dear Sammy Smith would volunteer
To call upon me in a trice,
  And pour his counsel in mine ear.
Still Sammy is, I must confess,
  About the biggest ass on earth ;—
So, gentle reader, you may guess
  What Smith's opinion would be worth.

"*RAIN, RAIN, GO AWAY!*"

FOR the Londoner leading a bachelor life
  There are miseries ample in store.
  There is want of a home, there is want of a
   wife ;
  There are millions of miseries more.
We have all many troubles and cares, I suppose,
 But I've this bitter truth to lay down—
That the worst of the woes a poor bachelor knows
 Is a very wet Sabbath in town.

When the morning is bright and the weather looks fair,
 You can take up your hat and your gloves,
And enliven your spirits by breathing the air
 In the haunts that a Londoner loves.
You may stroll as you list from the dawn to the dark
 When the sky has no signs of a frown ;—
But you cannot well visit Pall Mall or the Park
 On a very wet Sabbath in town.

When a friend (and a dear one) invites you to dine,
  You may laugh your depression to scorn;
You may chirrup with glee o'er his meats and his wine,
  And be happy till two in the morn.
But there stands not a hostel in merry Cockayne
  (Whatsoever its worth and renown),
Where the best of all dinners would not be in vain
  On a very wet Sabbath in town.

TO A LOVELY ACTRESS.

BRIGHT being, deign to listen to my hopes and
    to my fears,
    Though the homage of a multitude may linger
    in thine ears.
Thou hast earned a people's plaudits, and I doubt if
    thou canst care
For one fond heart's adoration—for one breaking
    heart's despair.

I have watched thee—how intently!—from the front
    row in the pit
(It is just about the centre that I generally sit).
Yesternight I saw thee smiling, but the smile was not
    for *me;*
Nay, I fear it was intended for the upper box, O. P.

I have witnessed thee in SHAKESPEARE, I have seen
    thee in burlesque
(I've a neat extravaganza nearly ready in my desk).
I was present on that evening when thy *début* took
    the town,
In a little farce of JONES's, and a comedy by BROWN.

Is it strange that I should love,thee? or particularly
    strange
I should ask thee for a trifle of affection in exchange?
Is it any fault of mine, too, that I *have* been married
    twice,
And my life is drawing quickly to the time of " second:
    price " ?

I cannot give thee rank or fame ; I cannot give thee
    gold ;
But richer far this trusting heart than opulence untold.
I cannot bring thee beauty ; but, as far as talent goes,
Why, I trust there *may* be intellect behind a turn-up
    nose !

Oh ! pardon me, adored one, for conveying thee a
    hint
Of the passion that consumes me—and for putting it
    in print.
If I publish my emotion, 'tis for all the world to see
That the tide of that emotion sets to thee—and *only*
    thee !

"DRIP! DRIP! DRIP!"

I.

AMONG the horrid acts we read
 Of Torquemada's Inquisition,
  I recollect a cruel deed
Befitting any fiend's commission.
The trick was very simply done :
 (True genius ever is adaptive !)
Mere water-drops fell one by one
  Plump on the cranium of the captive.

II.

'Twas quite refreshing first of all ;
 The heated brain found solace in it ;
But soon the thing began to pall,
 And made an age of every minute.
At length, to crown the dire effect
 Of this eternal patter-patter,
A man of giant intellect
 Became as mad as any hatter.

III.

Within our gentler modern life
  Such deeds could never find revival;
Yet in my true and loving wife
  Doth Torquemada boast a rival.
I never curse the cruel Fates
  Who brought me down to this condition:
I doat on her who emulates
  The late lamented Inquisition.

IV.

For her I sacrificed my Club—
  My pet resort—my seventh heaven;
To her I've yielded up my Chubb,
  And *must* be home before eleven.
I wear a pleased and placid grin,
  And strive to clank my fetters gaily:
Open revolt would be a sin,—
  But oh! the drops are dropping daily.

V.

She dreads tobacco—though the smell
  Is innocent, physicians tell us;
And, worst of all (I know it well),
  My lady is a little jealous.

Her fears are evidently vain,
   For banished is my mild Manilla ;
The cook's exceptionally plain,
   The housemaid is a she-gorilla.

VI.

Long years have I endured the rack
   From January to December.
One straw will break the camel's back,
   But that must be the *last*, remember.
Not many more can I survive
   Of paltry cares and petty trammels :
The end will very soon arrive ;
   My back is weaker than the camel's.

THROWN AWAY.

LINNET had perched on a myrtle spray
To idle its time in its own sweet way;
Innocent thing—defiant of capture—
Chirping a melody mad with rapture.
Oaks and ashes and elm-trees heard,
Nodding applause to the chanting bird;
The longer it sang the richer the plaudits
Paid by its woodland Court of Audits.

Still as the melody sank or swelled
It seemed that Nature her breathing held.
On a rose's petal a dewdrop glistened;
The dewdrop lingered, the wild rose listened.
Even the rivulet gliding past
Perhaps for the moment flowed less fast;
And the only lukewarm panegyric
Was that of the bard who writes this lyric.

For I am a Cockney, all in the dark
As to the linnet and as to the lark.
The oak and the ash and the elm-tree never
One from another can I dissever.
The song of the singer and all the glee
That it cast around were lost on *me.*
Less dear the notes of a woodland birdie
Than even a town-played hurdy-gurdy.

SUBLIMELY UNCONSCIOUS.

O the flowers of earth, to the stars above,
  To the sounding seas I have breathed my
      love.
I have hymned it morning and noon and night,
In poesy fit for a Bedlamite.
I have sung of my love to my Broadwood's grand ;
I have brooded upon it across the Strand—
Yet, bold as I am, I should hardly dare
To speak of my love to my lady fair.

The flowers were kind and the stars polite,
And the deep seas pitied my hopeless plight.
The verses I wrote were weak in rhyme ;
But they brought me joy for a brief, brief time.
My grand with my sorrows would oft condole,
And the Strand was dear to my Cockney soul.
I melted my listeners everywhere ;—
But could I have melted my lady fair ?

The flowers can fade, and the stars grow dim,
And the seas bring peril to life and limb;
And versification is oft a bore,
Unless for a guinea a line or more.
The pitch of my Broadwood's grand runs down.
There are prettier walks than the Strand in town.
So, altogether, I scarcely care
To risk the " No " of my lady fair.

TALES OF A GRANDFATHER.

GIDDY girls, you may laugh at your Grandpapa
   now,
      And enjoy putting pins in his chair;
Doubled up is this figure and furrowed this brow,
   Very scant are these teeth and this hair.
You may speak of me still in your soft pretty way
   As the quaintest old image unhung;
But a fond recollection survives my decay—
   I was very good-looking when young.

Half a century *does* make a sort of a kind
   Of a difference, mark you, my dears;
And the brief way to reckon my age up, I find,
   Is in tens or in dozens of years.
I must be about eighty or so, by the clock;
   But my mind is a little unstrung,
And my talent for counting has come to a block;—
   I was brilliant at figures when young.

In the dash-along hard-living Regency days
    I was prince of the fashion and style.
When I drove in the Park with my carriage and bays,
    Even Brummell bent low at my smile.
What was gold? A mere nothing. In pleasure and play
    Far and wide it got scattered and flung ;—
For, though now on the parish, I proudly can say
    I was rolling in riches when young.

Oh, the flirting and frolic and fun that we had!
    I was called an Adonis in curls.
There was many a feminine heart very sad
    When I married your Grandmother, girls.
I had rivals ; but what was a rival to *me*,
    With my figure, my face, and my tongue?
Ah, believe me, the squalid old pauper you see
    Was a dashing Don Juan when young.

DIFFICULT TO PLEASE.

I NEVER knew an uncle's love—an aunt's attentive care—
A first or second cousin whose emotions I could share ;
I've not one distant relative (by marriage or by birth)
To soothe me in my sadness, or to join me in my mirth.
My brothers and my sisters are as kind as they can be ;
I dote upon my parents, who are passing fond of *me*,
But I wish the Fates could manage—though I'm quite aware they can't—
To let me have an uncle, and some cousins, and an aunt !

If I could have a hundred pounds paid annually down,
And loving hearts about me in some cottage out of town—
Sequestered from the hum of men and Trade's eternal noise,
I'd spend my modest competence in Melibœan joys.

'Tis true that I am opulent—I live in regal state,
And pampered menials bring me food on gold and
    silver plate ;
Yet now and then I hanker for a pastoral career,
And think I might contrive it on a hundred pounds a
    year.

Could I produce a work of art to win a deathless
    name—
I mean a drama to arouse a multitude's acclaim—
How happily and proudly should I bow before the
    crowd,
While pit and gallery, box and stall, cried " Author ! "
    long and loud.
I've penned sensation articles and poems by the
    score—
I've written twenty novels ; or, it may be, rather more ;
And yet, amidst my triumphs, I occasionally sigh,
And murmur, " May I live to write a drama by and
    by ! "

If I were tall and slender, with a mane of auburn hue,
And if my nose were aquiline, and if my eyes were
    blue—
How carefully I'd cultivate Byronic looks and ways,
And make my hearers wonder with a foolish face of
    praise.

I'm only just the middle height (but not at all robust) ;
I'm highly prepossessing in appearance, as I trust ;
My eyes are big and brilliant, and my locks are black
    as jet;
Had I the pow'r of dyeing both, I might be happy yet.

CATCHING AT A STRAW.

HOUGH the planet of Love has grown dimmer
 And threatens to vanish outright,
Though the pale star of Hope gives a glimmer,
 And nought but a glimmer to-night;
Still my planet and star are above me,
 Still neither hath left me for good;
Though my loved one refuses to love me,
 She owns that she "would if she could."

They have bidden her think of another,
 She bends to the cruel command
Of a tyrannous father and mother,
 Who claim to dispose of that hand.
When I pleaded my depth of devotion
 She said—or I misunderstood—
That she dared not encourage the notion,
 But certainly "would if she could."

Shall I ever be happy, I wonder,
   With any one else for a wife?
No—the Fates that have torn us asunder
   Have left me a Cœlebs for life.
But one bright recollection may cheer me
   And shine on my bachelorhood;
Yes—my love, in declining to hear me,
   Confessed that she "would if she could."

PURE GRATITUDE.

I LED a life serenely gay,
  Without a shadow of a care.
    My only wants from day to day
  Were clothes and victuals, light and air.
But Love and Beauty forged me chains,
  And Cupid with his fond mamma
Turned all my pleasures into pains—
  Nous avons changé tout cela.

For *I* was young and very green,
  And *she* was young and very fair.
She marked my dignity of mien ;
  She praised my freely flowing hair.
'Twas all dishevelled, all unkempt,
  And yet it won her heart away.
From treating it with calm contempt,
  I've come to brush it ev'ry day.

She read my verses o'er and o'er,
   And thought they were extremely grand.
She read my essays, and she swore
   My prose betrayed a master hand.
That hand, so masterly before,
   Is getting cleaner now, I hope.
I wash it once a day, or more,
   With water and some honey-soap.

She loved my high poetic brow :
   I got a fifteen shilling hat.
'Tis damaged by the weather now
   To some extent—but what of that ?
My figure pleased her, for she thought
   My form as classic as my mind.
I went immediately and bought
   The loudest suit that I could find.

'Twas gratitude, and nothing less ;
   It made me prouder than a king
That she bewailed my loneliness,
   And smiled on such a wretched thing.
Our loves are dead ;—for good or ill
   A second life they gave to me.
I'm not respectable ; but still
   I'm better than I used to be.

MY NEIGHBOUR.

MORALIST, you lose your labour :
    Put your maxim on the shelf.
Nobody can love his neighbour
    As he loves his loving self.
Meek am I as any baby ;
    I've a temper of the best.
I could love my foe, it may be,
    But my neighbour I detest.

All my tastes are truly rural,
    So I sought a calm abode
In an Eden extramural—
    Number Nine, Amanda Road.
Fancy how my hopes were blighted
    When the noisiest of men,
By some wicked imp incited,
    Came to dwell at Number Ten.

Though the clerk of an attorney
    I'm an enemy to strife ;
I would make an easy journey
    All the way throughout my life.
How can life go very gaily
    (Either mine or other men's),
If a neighbour wakes you daily
    With a lot of cocks and hens ?

Ev'rybody has his hobby ;—
    Hydrophobia's one of mine,
Since our bravest local Bobby
    Perished from a bite canine.
When I pass my neighbour's gateway—
    Which I'd rather not, by half—
I expect his terrier straightway
    To detain me by the calf.

When at even, home returning—
    Worn and wearied through the day—
When for peace and quiet yearning,
    Still my neighbour stops the way.
Home will ever fail to cheer me,
    E'en in so retired a place,
While I have that fellow near me
    Practising the double-bass.

Reader, think me not a scorner
    Of the human race, I pray :
I am friends with round the corner,
    And I like across the way.
All the street—or very nearly—
    I converse with now and then ;
And could love my neighbour dearly,
    Were he aught but Number Ten !

"*FOR EVER!*"

A NOTE you sent me long ago,
  And long ago I fondly read it;
  And whether it was true or no,
For every word I gave you credit.
I have a notion that your note
  Was lively and a little clever;—
At present I can only quote
  Your final phrase of "Yours for ever!"

We deeply loved, I recollect;—
  We nursed a warm, undying passion;—
In short, we "spooned" with great effect
  In orthodox and proper fashion.
Our vows were not of such a kind
  As years can blot or seas can sever.
In all your letters ere you signed—
  You penned the phrase of "Yours for ever!"

That ardour is diminished now;
  'Tis rarely we exchange a letter;—
The tender past, we both allow,
  The sooner we ignore the better.
Our hopes are dead, our loves are o'er;
  I must forget them, now or never.—
Don't write me letters any more
  That end by saying "Yours for ever!"

A DREAM TO DREAM OF.

DREAMT a dream the other night—
　　When Slumber's poppy-chains had bound
　　　　me :—
Bright memories and hope as bright
　　Came crowding in a flock around me.
I bade adieu to real cares ;
　　I gave the slip to solid sorrows ;
And, buried in the night's affairs,
　　I never dreamt about the morrow's.

My feeble Fancy, so it seems,
　　Is nothing to be very vain of :
But now and then she brings me dreams
　　That I should love to dream again of.
I reckon, for its own sweet sake,
　　My dream of dreams among the number :
Methinks it was a shame to wake
　　In such a way from such a slumber.

I fear I cannot well portray
   The vivid features of my vision ;
To paint them in a prosy way,
   Would only be to court derision.
It strikes me, though as rather odd,
   (Through all my speculative scheming),
That—thanks to Morpheus, drowsy god—
   I never dreamt that I was dreaming.

A COMPROMISE.

HEN pleasures fly and hopes collapse,
    And cares are neither small nor few,
"To grin and bear it" is, perhaps,
    A philosophic thing to do.
I face Fortuna's bitter frown,
    And know repining is a sin.
When Disappointment hunts me down
    I bear it—but I cannot grin.

I've had my losses—who has not?
    In love and money, heart and purse.
Though discontented with my lot
    I feel there may be many worse.
I've met behaviour less than kind
    From folks that should be more than kin:
I say, "No matter: never mind!"—
    I bear it—but I cannot grin.

No, no ; the wise ones of the earth
   May tell me never to despair ;
May bid me with a mask of mirth
   Conceal the ravages of care.
Nay, rather let the gloom without
   Show something of the wreck within.
While Fate keeps pushing me about
   I bear it—but I cannot grin.

SYMPTOMS.

MY mem'ries take me back as early
　　As boyhood's green and gushing day;
These eyes were bright, these locks were
　　curly,
　And Life was lively as a play.
A change has long begun beginning,
　　And Life is as a tale twice-told;
My eyes are dimmed, my locks are thinning.
　　Can these be signs of growing old?

As lithe and active as a kitten
　　I joined the sports or led the dance.
You might have thought me badly bitten
　　By some Tarantula, perchance.
No more am I considered sportive—
　　Gout grips me in its iron hold—
My dancing efforts are abortive.
　　Can these be signs of growing old?

Belief I cultivated blindly
    In Jones and Robinson and Brown ;
And never could I judge unkindly
    One mortal in or out of town.
I should not nowadays be willing
    To credit Robinson with gold,
Or lend the other two a shilling.
    Can these be signs of growing old ?

Once Angelina seemed angelic—
    I fancied Fanny quite a dear;
Of each I treasured up a relic
    From day to day and year to year.
Their faces I can scarce remember,
    For Time has turned my passions cold,
Love's May has lapsed in Love's December.
    Can these be signs of growing old ?

What wonder I am weary-hearted,—
    What marvel that it clouds my brow,
To think of what has long departed,
    And think of what is left me now ?
The bitter truth is past concealing,—
    The more my symptoms I unfold
The more confirmed becomes the feeling,
    That these *are* signs of growing old.

MOCK MODESTY.

FEW of the fellows that come to the Club
    Are excessively modest though garrulous
      people ;
    Each gives his own merits a sneer or a snub
To exalt those of others as high as a steeple.
For any one loving—as *I* do—a lark,
    'Tis as good as a play when they cackle together.
I never would willingly miss a remark
    That escapes these ingenuous " birds of a feather.'

Poor X., let us say, brings a comedy out ;—
    But the critical press (which is awfully cruel)
Seems rather in doubt what the plot is about,
    So it gives the unfortunate author his " gruel."
He smiles at the worst that his critics can say,
    And observes that for taste there is now no account-
      ing.
He bashfully begs you to sit through his play
    For its exquisite acting and elegant mounting.

1

Poor Y., a musician with scraps of a voice,
 Is declared by the Club undeniably clever ;—
In fact, I imagine the Club would rejoice
 Could he warble away at its Collard for ever.
He mildly but firmly denies he can sing ;
 And he blushes when any one tries to *encore* him ;
It seems, he asserts, a most marvellous thing
  That the Peerage admire and the Public adore
   him.

Poor Z. is a poet—a promising bard—
 But is under that curse of the poet's condition
Which doometh him—struggle he never so hard—
 To ignore the delights of a second edition.
He owns a great army of pressmen as friends,
 And the notices penned on his labours are glowing.
Those choice gems of intellect make him amends
  For the coldness the masses at large have been
   showing.

Our nature has phases most comic to meet,
 But I vow and protest the absurdest and oddest
Is found when humility covers conceit
 And inordinate vanity apes being modest.
Our Club is the brightest and best ever seen,
 For our Club is composed of intelligent fellows ;—
But, somehow or other, they look very mean
  When they live upon puffs out of other men's
   bellows.

THE GENTLE SHEPHERD.

HARK how Corydon and Chloe
  Greet us with a merry song !
  I'll be Strephon—you be Zoe ;
   Let us join their giddy throng.
In the mead or by the grotto
Dwell with me, love, *à la Watteau.*

When our daily work is over,
  (Only work to suit the lazy !)
Be it ours to live in clover—
  Or in buttercup—or daisy.
Far niente be our motto ;
Dream with me, love, *à la Watteau.*

Fast the dancers go and faster—
  Arlecchino in the middle.—
Perched aloft, as ballet-master,
  Pierrot nimbly scrapes the fiddle.
Would you miss the gay ridotto ?
Dance with me, love, *à la Watteau.*

Come, a carol !   Sure 'twere pity
    Leaving incomplete the frolic;
Sing some old Parisian ditty,
    Pseudo-classico-bucolic ;—
Light as Offenbach or Flotow,
Chant with me, love, *à la Watteau.*

When the night shall close around us—
    When the dance and song are quiet—
We shall have a supper found us
    Of the best Italian diet.—
Maccaroni and risotto
Eat with me, love, *à la Watteau.*

SEPTEMBER IN TOWN.

SUMMER is ended, and Autumn is here—
    Though for the present we're not very far in
      it.
    Oysters are back again—awfully dear:
Still they are back, for the month has an R in it.
Leaves will be shortly beginning to fall
    Thick o'er the Parks as the snow on the Jura lies.
When shall I fly—if I *can* fly at all—
    Far from the bricks and the mortar to ruralise?

Nobody here to be met by or meet;—
    Long have I grown of the terrible truth aware;
Long have I wandered in square and in street,
    Desolate now as the walls of Balclutha were.
Blame not the bard if a desert so bare
    Pains him to think of it—hurts him to speak of it.
Pity the plaint of his utter despair;—
    "Oh! for the country, if only a week of it."

Barely a line in a day can I write ;
   Barely a line, either prosy or lyrical.
Dozens, when London is full, I indite—
   Pleasantly morbid or mildly satirical.
Trained in the country a poet should be ;—
   Coleridge, and Wordsworth, and ever so many were.
Why not at once make a poet of *me ?*—
   Somebody—take me—directly—to anywhere !

MY BOTTLES.

THEY speak to me of other days
   And mutely suffered pain ;
   They move my heart in many ways,
And move it not in vain.
Upon my shelf, against my wall,
   I range them in a row ;
And murmur " Bless ye, one and all,
   Dear friends of long ago ! "

There's not a label in the lot
   But has a tale to tell ;
Nor one that I remember not,
   And can't remember well.
And gloomily on gloomy days
   I love to sit and pore
Upon the ne'er-forgotten phrase,
   " The mixture as before."

My own is not a healthy mind,
   But broods upon disease ;
And nowhere could I hope to find
   Companions fit as these.
One bottle brings me back a cough ;
   One brings me back a cold ;
And one a fever warded off
   By tonics manifold.

Go, call them empty if ye will ;—
   This philosophic brain
Can easily contrive to fill
   Those bottles once again—
Those bottles fill with all the fears
   And all the hopes of yore ;
Till even Life itself appears
   A " mixture as before."

AN APHORISM.

YEARS ago, in my days of school,
    I fell in a fury twice an hour.
    (Years ago I was half a fool,
        And foolery made and kept me sour.)
Riper and wiser age has brought
    This axiom, simple and yet sublime ;
Nothing is worth one angry thought,
    For loss of temper is loss of time.

All experience tends to teach
    The best and the worst of mortal men,
How the limits of life will reach
    Only to threescore years and ten.
Life is made of a million parts,
    And waste of life is a kind of crime.
Why these passionate fits and starts,
    Since loss of temper is loss of time ?

I've my enemies, Goodness knows—
   Who can exist without a few?
Secret slanderers, open foes;
   Ready for all that spite can do.
Let them chatter from dawn till eve;
   By day or by night, from chime to chime,
I hold my peace for I still believe
   That loss of temper is loss of time.

TRICKS OF THE TRADE.

I CONFESS that I feel an apology due
    To the public who feast on my rhymes ;
    Many things that I've written are grossly untrue,
  Though I've stated them dozens of times.
I regret it ; I never will do so again ;
  My resolves for the future are made.
I will worship the truth, and for ever disdain
  To indulge in the tricks of the trade.

I have told ye, my public, of Poverty's pangs ;
  Of the crust and the pallet of straw ;—
And the Demon of Want with its pitiless fangs
  Have I often made efforts to draw.
What a lark !—I am rich ; I've a thousand a year,
  'Twas a practical joke that I played.
Did I summon a sigh ; did I call up a tear?
  It was only a trick of the trade.

With my quip and my crank, with my joke and my
    song,
  I am first among jesters and wits.
It is only when *solus*, away from the throng,
  That I've hypochondriacal fits.
All alive where the light of society beams,
  I may droop now and then in the shade ;
But my moods of depression are brief as my dreams—
  Though of use as a trick of the trade.

I've remarked, and perhaps in a querulous tone,
  That I thought it a sin and a shame
For a poet of promise to linger unknown
  When he courts recognition and fame.
Did you fondly suppose that I spoke for myself?
  I have laurels that never can fade.
You, my public, have some of my lines on your shelf—
  It was merely a trick of the trade.

I have told you, no doubt, that I rarely was well ;
  That my frame was a mass of disease.
Little fibs of the sort are so easy to tell,
  And in verse are so certain to please.
But I'll cut the concern, my transgressions are o'er,
  The apology due has been paid.
Pen and ink, I devote ye to Truth evermore,
  And abandon the tricks of the trade.

WHAT I WANT.

I WANT a heart—one heart alone,
 To beat responsive to mine own.
  Go, Fate, and look for one—and find it ;
 Or, if you cannot, never mind it.

I want—what magic in the sounds !—
About one hundred thousand pounds,
But shall I get the sum ? I doubt it ;
So let me push along without it.

I want a mansion in a square,
Or in a park, or anywhere.
Go, Fate, and find it in a hurry—
But stay, I won't be such a worry.

I want a fitter state of mind,
Much more contented and resigned :—
Then Fancy in her free expansion
May bring the money, heart, and mansion.

THE PARROT AND THE CAT.

I'VE a deep domestic tragedy that calls for your
     attention,
    If your sympathy a minute you'll be good
      enough to grant ;
And, by way of a beginning to my story, I may mention
    That a year or so ago, you know, I had a maiden-
     aunt.
I was constant in my visits to her hospitable dwelling
    For a quiet cup of coffee and a comfortable chat.
She possessed a mint of money—and the fact is worth
     my telling,
    That she also had a parrot, and she also had a cat.

I confess that I grew jealous, for my aunt was deeply
     smitten
    With her biped and her quadruped and all their
     pretty tricks ;

She had known the cat and loved it ever since it was
    a kitten,
    She had known and loved the parrot when the bird
    was under six.
And the beast was very clever, and the bird was very
    funny ;
    For the bird was good at language, and the beast
    was good at rats ;
But I hardly liked the notion that my aunt should
    leave her money
    To an hospital for parrots or dispensary for cats.

So I seized an opportunity whenever I could get it
    To instruct these hated animals in very wicked
    ways ;
Pretty Poll was very rapid at the lessons that I set it,
    Pretty Pussy was a pupil to deserve the highest
    praise.
If you ever heard a sailor speak the dialect of
    Wapping,
    I assure you that the parrot spoke a little worse
    than *that ;*
And it's only very rarely that you find a creature
    dropping
    Into such abandoned habits as that miserable
    cat.

When I found myself the master of this noble
    situation,
  I would gladly paint my joy, you know (although,
    you know, I can't);
And a month or so ago, you know, I heard with
    resignation
  That I'd lost a friend and relative;—I mean my
    maiden-aunt.
When the lady's will and testament was read by her
    attorney
  I was naturally present, with a crape about my hat:
I was paid for all my trouble and rewarded for my
    journey
  By a legacy consisting of—the Parrot and the Cat!

(Sung by MR. GEORGE GROSSMITH, junior, by whom the music
has been composed.)

CONFUSION!

I WROTE a note an hour ago
    To Snip of Piccadilly.
  "Dear Sir," said I, "to dun me so
    Is obstinate and silly."
Referring to an old account,
  I begged him to be lenient;
For I would pay the small amount
  As early as convenient.

I wrote a note an hour ago
  To sweet Matilda Marshall
(To whom, as many of you know,
  The bard is very partial).
I crammed the paper full of love,
  Four pages full of passion;
And cooed like any turtle-dove
  In true poetic fashion.

K

Capricious Fate (who ever gloats
 When bards get into messes)
Contrived that these impressive notes
 Got mixed in their addresses.
Ay, that's the trouble—there's the rub :
 The horrible suggestion :—
While sweet Matilda gets a snub,
 To Snip I've popped the question.

AN UNEQUAL MATCH.

I MET a damsel in a dream,
  With sunny locks—ah, such a gleam!
  With eyes that pierced me through and through
At ev'ry glance—ah, such a hue!
In waking hours my dream again
Returns to bring me joy and pain.—
Ah, why was I a lowly churl,
And she the offspring of an Earl?

I vainly prayed that cruel Fate
Would lift me to some higher state—
Some situation far above
The one in which I nursed my love.
I dared not breathe my love aloud;
His Lordship was austere and proud.—
Ah, why was I a lowly churl,
And she the offspring of an Earl?

To share my meek and humble cot
Would scarce have seemed her fitting lot.
Those haughty oligarchs, they say,
Insist on dining ev'ry day.
She might have deemed it *infra dig.*
To milk my cow or tend my pig.—
Ah, why was I a lowly churl,
And she the offspring of an Earl?

It would have been my doom, no doubt,
Sometimes to be invited out;
To feast with noblemen, perchance,
Or join a Countess in the dance.
My manly form, I must confess,
Would be at sea in evening dress.—
Ah, why was I a lowly churl,
And she the offspring of an Earl?

To-night—as bedward I repair,
And slowly scale my garret stair—
I mean to pray, " O Sleep ! restore
The dream you gave me once before.
Bring back my love—bring back my prize ;
Her form and face, her locks and eyes ;—
Make *me* the offspring of an Earl,
And *her* a lowly peasant girl."

THE SUPER'S DREAM.

I'VE played at the West, and I've played in the
    City;
    But never got on with my managers yet.
On my honour I think—and I think it's a pity—
    They're jealous and stingy, the whole of the set.
They allow I perform in a praiseworthy manner,
    And own I'm a fairly respectable man,
Yet insist upon sending me on with a banner;—
    And *why?*—Let them answer me that, if they can.

And why at the tail of my craft should I linger,
    On salaries less than it suits me to name;
When I feel that one flourish from Fate's little finger
    At once could promote me to riches and fame?
I behold in my visions a dim panorama,
    Processions heroic in panoply grand;—
And in all the great parts in the classical drama
    My own *alter ego*—-myself second-hand !

Too fugitive dreams !—It was one of their number
    That beamed on my sadness a fortnight ago.—
(Happy mortals inherit full often in slumber
    More pleasure than mortals awake ever know.)
But the annals of Dreamland a rapture can tell not—
    A bliss more ecstatic—a joy more serene ;
For my manager, SOMNUS, had cast me for Melnotte,
    And lovely Matilda MacTabb for Pauline.

Ah me—how my heart with ambition was burning !—
    Ah me—how my pulses with energy beat !—
There was no indecision whatever concerning
    The way to dispose of my hands and my feet.
O'er this bosom young Love with Apollo stood sentry,
    To guard me from all that could mar my success.
I mistook not one exit, I missed not one entry ;
    And never confounded O.P. with P.S.—

The love of Matilda MacTabb had inspired me ;—
    I ranted—I bullied—I swindled—I fought—
And, in fact, I did all that my author desired me ;
    Which means that I did pretty much what I ought.
But alas !—I had studied five acts to discover
    That SOMNUS had played me a practical joke :
For ere the Pauline—[my MacTabb]—and her lover
    Could make up their minds to be wedded—I woke !

MUCH TOO KIND.

I'M the soul of good-nature, and make it my aim
    To oblige all the world when I can :
  And, wherever Society utters my name,
  I am known as " that willing young man."
But our merits are faults when they run to excess,
  As I'll try in two minutes to show.
I have learned for so long to say nothing but Yes
  That I never could learn to say No.

People ask me to sing, or to play, or to dance,
  Or to join them at cribbage or whist;
I would rather decline, but they see at a glance
  That I dare not and cannot resist.
People borrow my coin in their affable style,
  From a crown to a fiver or so :
And I lend with a smile, but regret all the while
  That I never could learn to say No.

To go shopping with ladies I'm daily required,
    Or to stroll in the Park or the " Zoo " ;—
And they seem to imagine I never grow tired,
    Though I beg to remark that I *do*.
To a play or a concert, a party or ball,
    'Tis my destiny nightly to go :
For of course my tormentors have learnt one and all
    That I never could learn to say No.

When my time and my money both come to an end,
    At the close of my earthly career,
Let me go to my grave as Humanity's Friend,
    For my rights to the title are clear.
Let my epitaph run to the modest effect
    That the gentleman lying below
Was perfection in all but one little respect—
    That he never could learn to say No !

STANZAS.

TO A THOUGHTLESS ONE.

MY hair is gray, but not with years—
    Despair has bleached my tresses,
    Since you (the source of all my tears'
  Rejected my addresses.
The flame that made my bosom smart
  Was bright and clear and steady ;
I only strove to touch your heart,—
  Your brain was touched already.

I told you how my passion burned,—
  I breathed my true devotion ;—
I murmured, " Is my love returned ? "—
  You hardly had a notion.
Yet still I pined the truth to find,
  My chance looked not a bad one :
You talked of making up your mind,
  Until I thought you *had* one.

Alas ! you smiled on other chaps,
   And came at length to doubt me :
Not having thoughts enough, perhaps,
   To spare a thought about me.
Farewell !   I break the fatal charm,
   And quit you as you bid me ;
I think you never *meant* me harm,
   But oh ! the harm you *did* me.

METROPOLITAN IMPROVEMENTS.

BY AN OBSTRUCTIVE.

WHERE'ER we wander—up or down—
 They still go on improving ;
The only cry o'er all the town
 Is, " Push along ! Keep moving ! "
For architecture wins the day,
 And celebrates her glories
By palaces that line the way
 With six or seven storeys.

The haunts we revelled in to-day
 We lose to-morrow morning ;
As one by one are swept away
 In turn without a warning.
Alas ! while progress, at a touch,
 Commits new devastations,
Our old resorts we miss as much
 As elderly relations.

Ah, when shall we again pursue
 Our rambles and researches—
As once it was a joy to do—
 Among the City churches?
Those fanes have hardly left a trace
 To go in loving quest of;—
Our new-built City is a place
 That Mammon has the best of.

No longer we with pleasure plod
 Our way by Covent Garden,
To meditate as if we trod
 Some Cockney path in Arden.
We cannot call within our ken
 The homes of *Will* and *Button;*—
The coffee-houses, like the men,
 Are gone as dead as mutton.

No nook or cranny dear to me
 Should undergo removal,
Though Progress went on either knee
 To beg for my approval.
There's Temple Bar! I only know
 That hundreds will regret it,
Supposing that it has to go :—
 Still—if it *must*—why, let it!

TRUE FRIENDSHIP.

WHEN a scamp disappears from this region of
      woe
    The survivors infallibly hear
That, excepting his own, he was nobody's foe ;—
  An expression more touching than clear.
O'er the tomb of old Higgins 'twere fitter by far
  That the sculptor should carve on a stone—
After stating what all the particulars are—
   "He was nobody's friend but his own."

Uncle Higgins, with numbers of thousands a year,
  Is of course a most excellent man ;
Which is more than they think of his nephew, I fear,
  With his hundred and fifty *per ann.*
Does old Higgins come down with his dust ?   Not a
   sou ;
  Nay, the older old Higgins has grown
The more strictly he renders that epitaph true—
   "He was nobody's friend but his own."

But with pluck and with patience I somehow get on,
    And exist by the help of my brains ;
While I wait for the time when old Higgins is gone
    To a world where no currency reigns.
Should his last will and testament show some design
    For his many past sins to atone,
I could curb my resentment and cancel the line—
    "He was nobody's friend but his own."

AN EXCUSE FOR EVERYTHING.

HERE is merit in open confession, they say;
    So I cheerfully pander to truth
    By admitting at once that I still am a prey
    To some pleasant illusions of youth.
I shall change for the better, no doubt, by degrees,
    And in time be less gushing and green.
Laugh away at my errors as much as you please;
    But remember—I'm only eighteen.

To the friends that have brightened my pathway in
    life
    What a depth of devotion I owe!
They are guiltless of hatred, of malice, of strife,
    Or of sentiment selfishly low.
What a darling is Jones, what an angel is Brown;
    What a trump has young Robinson been!—
I may learn in the future, to run them all down;
    But at present—I'm only eighteen.

I have grown, I confess it, a slave to the fair—
  Led astray by the first pretty face;
And, if Love be indeed a delusion—a snare,—
  You may pity, not envy, my case.
If I worship a score of the sex at a time,
  An excuse can be readily seen;
I will say to the censor who counts it a crime,
  Stop a moment!—I'm only eighteen.

I believe, and I fancy that others believe,
  To be rich is in truth to be great.
With a thousand a year for my life, I conceive
  I could live in comparative state.
The delights of a fortune I grasp at a glance,
  And the joys that a fortune may mean.
I shall make one by fifty, or sixty, perchance;
  But I've told you—I'm only eighteen.

When my style has been strengthened and polished
    a bit,
  I will burst on the wondering world
With a brain full of eloquence, wisdom, and wit,
  And the banner of genius unfurled.
I'm simply delaying on purpose to find
  How my talent and sympathy lean.
Only stop till I've thoroughly made up my mind—
  There's no hurry—I'm only eighteen.

"*SHOP!*"

HATEVER you sell, Sir—whatever you
  trade in—
  I hope I may mildly but firmly suggest
That, as well as the time all your profits are made in,
 Enough is allowed you for natural rest.
No doubt the excitements of Commerce are thrilling,
 'Tis hard from such altitudes ever to drop ;—
But, at least for to-night, Sir—however unwilling—
 Do put up your shutters and shut up your shop.

You see, Sir, I too am a tradesman and brother,
 As greedy for gain as the best of my crew ;—
Only *I* offer one thing, and *you* sell another,
 And neither imagines he's worst of the two.
Of course there is nothing of rivalry in it,
 Where each has a tree and inhabits the top ;—
Still, by way of a novelty,—just for a minute—
 Pray put up your shutters and shut up your shop.

Just fancy the state of affairs at a meeting
　　Of traders in ev'ry conceivable trade;
One and all in a frenzy, with fury repeating
　　The fact that their goods were the best ever made.
A picture so ghastly should act as a warning.—
　　This mercantile maundering try, Sir, to stop;
And, until you get ready for work in the morning,
　　Please put up your shutters and shut up your shop.

STRICTLY PRACTICAL.

IT is easy, no doubt, in a ballad or novel
    To write about money as rubbish or dust;
  It is easy to picture young Love in a hovel
      Subsisting on water combined with a crust.
Common sense gives a different view to the question,
  Let songster or novelist write as he may;
And a palace, if bards will excuse the suggestion,
  Is not an unpleasant abode in its way.

To be caged in a cottage and starve like a Stoic,
  To plod for a pittance of little or less,
May be highly romantic and rather heroic,
  But cannot precisely be pleasant, I guess.
I declare I could love in as fervid a fashion
  If lodged in the building by Buckingham Gate;
With a view of the Park to intensify passion,
  And food of the best on the richest of plate.

So I mildly but firmly present my denial
　To novels and songs upon Indigent Love ;
And I promise hereby, if you'll grant me the trial,
　To revel in riches and coo like a dove.
But my life in the future (though married and
　　wealthy)
　Depends very much on the bride that I win ;—
Make me clever, good-looking, good-natured, and
　　healthy,
　And bring me a Duchess and let me begin.

BACK AT SCHOOL.

RUANT heart and idle brain
  Aid me in my toil again.
  Long ye both have been astray
Keeping pleasant holiday.
Ye have stayed an age together,
Basking in the sunny weather.
School is open once again :—
Help me, heart, and help me, brain.

As for you, my fickle heart,
Finely have you played your part.
Emma Jane and Mary Ann
Must release you if they can.
Long as you have been a rover,
Now the time for play is over ;
You have surely had your fling,—
Back to school, you giddy thing.

Brain, I rather think that *you*
Are the lazier of the two.
You of sport have had your share,
Here and there and everywhere.
Bid adieu awhile to funning,
And assist me with your cunning.
Come and finish all the rhyme
Left neglected such a time !

BRADSHAW'S GUIDE.

AIR—*The Devil among the Tailors.*

DID you ever?—No, you never—dreamt of such
absurdities—
Enough to make your noddle ache—it is,
upon my word it is ;
A handy thing for travelling I've pretty often heard it
is,
And so I've been investing in a " Bradshaw's
Guide."
But what with all the figures to be hunting up or
diving at,
And what with all your efforts to discover what
they're driving at—
The stations you are leaving, or the places you're
arriving at,
I'm hanged if you can fathom in a " Brad-
shaw's Guide."

In a fuss you mount a 'bus, which article vehicular
Is very slow—because, you know, the driver's not
particular—

" Do look alive ; how slow you drive ! " you shout in
his auricular ;
"My train's eleven-twenty by my ' Brad-
shaw's Guide ! ' "
Arriving at the station in a fuming and a flurrying,
You find a lot of passengers all hurrying and
skurrying ;
Old ladies and old gentlemen are bothering and
worrying
For bits of information out of " Bradshaw's
Guide."

In your book you take a look, to see how far your
station is,
Begin to doubt, on finding out how tough the
explanation is ;
And when you've read until your head in utter
agitation is,
You've not a high opinion of your " Brad-
shaw's Guide."
The startings and the stoppages have taxed my own
urbanity,
Until my mighty intellect is verging on insanity ;
If any book was ever yet a torture to humanity,
Decidedly the volume is a " Bradshaw's
Guide."

DOUBT AND DECISION.

1.

MY mind is dubious, dreary, dark,—
　　Not a glimpse of day, not a sunbeam spark.
　　No making it up to confront a question
Unsolved for want of a mere suggestion.
All is mystery, all is gloom ;
The organ of thought is a darkened room.
The window down and the blind pulled closely,
And somewhere a figure that broods morosely.

II.

Got it at last !　By Jove, what fun !—
Clear as the noonday ; clear as the sun.
What was I dreaming about, I wonder ?—
What wild fit was I labouring under ?
Something I took to eat or drink
Made such a hash of my brains, I think.
Well, no matter !　I've made my mind up ;—
Open the window and pull the blind up.

SELF-DENIAL.

THE most unselfish man am I
    That ever was created :
And if you think this truth a lie,
    Just hear it demonstrated.
Let four-and-twenty hours go round
    On any clock or dial ;
And still, wherever I am found,
    I study self-denial.

Whene'er I see an oyster-shop,
    If I obeyed my wishes,
I tell you frankly, I should stop
    To taste the little fishes ;
My purse is empty, and I feel
    That hunger is a trial ;
But proudly I forego the meal,
    And study self-denial.

Within my heart, a while ago,
  Young CUPID came to lord it:
But am I wedded? Bless you, no!
  I never could afford it.
And, though my merit may escape
  The cynic's cold espial,
I think that in its noblest shape
  I study self-denial.

If any luxury is dear,
  I never stay to buy it:
If any task is too severe,
  I scarcely ever try it.
Though Fate may empty on my head
  The wrath of every vial,
I trust it will at least be said
  I study self-denial.

THE STAGE DOOR.

I STOOD by the door at the noontide hour,
    With an armful of dog's-eared paper;
    Long over a play. of undoubted pow'r
I had wasted the nightly taper.
And I wanted the manager once for all
    To reject the thing or accept it.
I had shown it to managers great and small,
    And had carried it home and kept it.

I fell into love while I dangled there
. (As a poor-devil author dangles)
With a pretty princess, who looked so fair
    By night in her silks and spangles.
'Twas love at first sight for each and both;
    But my life was a strife so lonely
That I thought it a sin to plight my troth
    For love and for true love only.

I stood by day and I stood by night,
   When the weather was none the clearest ;
As an author who struggles to see the light,
   As a lover who seeks his dearest.
But my life to-day is a sunnier life
   (So my rhyme has a tinge of reason)—
For the pretty princess is my own dear wife,
   And my drama ran all the season.

A SLAVE TO CIRCUMSTANCES.

A MORE disreputable hound—
　　A more degraded castaway—
　　Was never met with, I'll be bound,
Than—Tommy Smith, suppose we say.
He tells me that he *might* have grown
　　Renowned, respectable, and rich;
But every chance was overthrown
　　By "circumstances over which,
　　　　　　　　Et cetera!"

Poor Tommy started in the race
　　Ambitious of a poet's name;
And struggled long to find a place
　　Amongst the favourites of Fame.
She slammed her door in Tommy's face,
　　When he implored an empty niche:
Poor Smith attributes his disgrace
　　To "circumstances over which,
　　　　　　　　Et cetera!"

Unhappy in his wedded life,
    He's rather given, I believe,
To beat his children and his wife
    From dawn until the dewy eve.
But if his troubles (not a few)
    Have led poor Smith to such a pitch,
Small weaknesses like this are due
    To "circumstances over which,
                Et cetera !"

He has a tendency to drink
    (Not only when he dines or sups);
His language, too, is on the brink
    Of "shady," when he's in his cups.
He wanders idly o'er the town,
    And speaks of dying in a ditch;
And, when he *does*, he'll set it down
    To "circumstances over which,
                Et cetera !"

MY BIRD.

ONG ago I loved, alas !
 Loved a lass and very truly.
 On a day it came to pass
That I made an offer duly.
Sinking on my knees I fired
 Sighs and simpers in a volley ;—
Fondly, madly I aspired
 To the hand of pretty Polly.

Rapture, ecstasy, delight !—
 "Yes" was all my Mary uttered ;
But a mist was o'er my sight,
 And my heart with ardour fluttered.
Yet within a little week,
 Urged by frenzy or by folly,
I was flirting with a "cheek"
 That amazed my pretty Polly.

She returned the little things
    Sent as proofs of my affection ;
Chains, and photographs, and rings,
    Rather a unique collection !
Then my heart grew sick and sad.—
    Flirting may be very jolly ;
Still my goings on were bad
    As regarded pretty Polly.

Conscience, that ill-omened bird,
    Morning, noon and even haunts me ;
Day and night its cry is heard,
    And the ghostly echo taunts me.
When I'm brooding all alone,
    Sulky, sad, and melancholy,
Still I hear its parrot tone
    Ever crowing "pretty Polly !"

GOOD COMPANY.

AT evening in the winter time
    I love to nestle near the fire,
   At leisure polishing a rhyme,
  Or dozing to my heart's desire.
Then, let it blow, or snow, or freeze,
  The rain may stream along the street;
I little care while well at ease
  Within my snug and safe retreat.

Should rhyme and reverie grow flat,
  I take a volume off my shelf;
And institute a cosy chat
  Between its author and myself.
Should *he* become a dreary guest,
  I straight invite a dozen more
(My library is quite a nest
  Of ancient and of modern lore).

I call my Shelley or my Pope,
  My Burns, my Dryden, or my Keats ;
Or, should I seek a higher scope,
  My Milton here my Shakespeare meets.
For prose I summon Dicky Steele,
  Mild Addison, or burly Sam ;
Or, coming later down, appeal
  To Hazlitt, Hunt, or Charley Lamb.

In Space's and in Time's despite,
  They come from ev'ry clime and age.
With some I talk for half a night,
  With some for only half a page.
Such clever folks !—I fancy, though,
  My pow'rs of thought their own excel ;
For *they* have told me all they know,
  And all *I* know I never tell.

AMBITION'S YEARNINGS.

ET me ask your advice, Mr. Editor, pray—
    On a matter that robs me of rest;
    It annoys me by night and it haunts me by
      day,
  Till I seem like a person possest.
I am wildly ambitious and burn for a name;
  And in arms or in art or in song,
On my word and my honour, I think I should claim
  A well-merited place before long.
        I wish to be famous, I wish to be great.
        Can I manage to do it, or am I too late?

I should like to commence, Mr. Editor, sir—
  As a poet, a *vates*, a bard,
The Miltonic (or blank) is the verse I prefer,
  As I fancy that rhyming is hard.
May I beg you to tell me how much (money down)
  It would cost me to come out in print?
Would an epic on Charlemagne tickle the town?
  I should feel so obliged for a hint.
        I wish to be famous, I wish to be great.
        Can I manage to do it, or am I too late?

The musicians are making a noise in the world,
   And for music I'd always a thirst.
The romantic and classical flags are unfurl'd,
   And I'm eager to fight for the first.
Shall I risk a recital and play through a list
   From Talexy, Ganz, Ascher, and Strauss ?
I believe my expression and firmness of wrist
   Would be certain to draw me a house.
        I wish to be famous, I wish to be great.
        Can I manage to do it, or am I too late ?

After all, very likely "the play is the thing,"
   As the sweet Swan of Avon observes.
I've a drama prepared that would act like a spring
   On the lachrymal duct and the nerves.
Never doubt it will prove a colossal success ;
   And I hope, Mr. Editor, *you*
And your many good friends on the critical press
   Will be ready with all you can do.
        I wish to be famous, I wish to be great.
        Can I manage to do it, or am I too late ?

I have told you my troubles and opened my heart ;—
   Now I nervously wait a reply.
Any gems of advice that you please to impart
   I shall treasure, of course, till I die.

I repeat, I shall value as long as I live
   Whatsoever you choose to confide ;—
Only whether I act on the lessons you give
   Is a matter for *me* to decide.
       ·I wish to be famous, I wish to be great.
       Can I manage to do it, or am I too late ?

A MARTYR.

"I can't get out!"—Sterne's Sentimental Journey.

YORICK heard thee, pretty starling,
    And on one undying page
    Fixed thy plaint, my little darling,
    While it fluttered from thy cage.
Yes, the tender Yorick heard thee
    With a sympathy devout,
When captivity had stirred thee
    To the cry, "I can't get out."

Thus the words became historic;
    Thus will they continue so.
Ah, that *I* possessed a Yorick
    To perpetuate my woe.
Free as air my friends are flying
    Here and there and far about;
Nought remains for me but sighing,
    Like thyself, "I can't get out."

Some are deep amongst the heather,
　　Some are sailing on the sea.
All—to take them altogether—
　　Are as happy as can be.
Save in summer, London City
　　Has a charm, without a doubt;
Still in summer one may pity
　　Him who sighs " I can't get out."

TO A COQUETTE.

HOW often have you told me, dear,
    That patience is a virtue!
I'm nearly out of it, I fear,
    You flighty little flirt, you.
I mean to throw your chains away,
    And fit some other set on;
Forgetting that unlucky day—
    The day that first we met on.

I mean to play a bolder part,
    And (slowly, dear, but surely)
Win back the lacerated heart
    You thought your own securely.
The toy I take away from you
    Elsewhere will be presented;
And still may look as good as new
    If properly cemented.

I'll send you back your lock of hair—
    Your photograph (untinted) ;
It made you younger than you were,
    As I've already hinted.
I'll send your letters, ev'ry note ;—
    Why, folks would hardly credit
The sprawly, peaky hand you wrote—
    And yet I always read it.

Those brooches and the little rings—
    You may as well return them.
My letters, too, the silly things—
    I think I'd better burn them.
Farewell !—and yet we *must* contrive
    One meeting ere we sever.
I'll call to-morrow, then, at five,
    To say " Adieu for ever ! "

THE NIGHT-GUARDS.

"OH, tell me, tell me, mother mine,
    What sounds are those that break the
        stillness?"
Thus asked a boy of eight or nine,
    Still weak from very recent illness.
"Oh, tell me; for methinks I hear
    The clash of arms, my mother dear."

The mother listened for a while;
    Two briny tears bedimmed her lashes;
She heard the step of rank and file
    Of subalterns in showy sashes.
'Twas vain to chide the starting tear;—
Her husband was a Grenadier.

On either side the street there went
    Stern men with guns upon their shoulders.
All pale—but resolute—they bent
    Knit brows upon the scared beholders.
Amidst the troops (towards the rear)
The matron marked her Grenadier.

"Sleep, child," she muttered; "sleep to-night,
   Thy father will return to-morrow.
At duty's voice, till morning's light
   He leaves me to thyself and sorrow.
At glory's call defying fear,
He goes to guard the Bank, my dear.

"To guard the grim and lonely pile,
   And keep secure the sombre portals
Against the foes of Britain's isle,
   Or British but nefarious mortals.
The night is long—the night is drear;
But father is a Grenadier.

"To Drury Lane another band
   Will march with dauntless resolution,
And, fully armed, for hours will stand
   Before that Thespian institution."
"O mother!" shrieked the boy in fear,
"I would not be a Grenadier!"

DAY AND NIGHT.

THERE are days without a pleasure,
   There are nights without a star.
  There are times when all the treasure
   Of our hopes has flown afar.
But the day is quickly over,
  And a night is quickly past,
And the hope that is a rover
  May return to us at last.

If the day forbids the flowing
  Of our bitter tears to cease,
There is comfort in the knowing
  That the night will bring us peace.
In a night of sad endurance,
  In the darkness of our pain,
We have ever the assurance
  That the dawn will come again.

As the night will bring its morrow,
  And the morrow bring its night,
So the seasons of our sorrow
  Bring the seasons that are bright.
So the day will soon be over,
  And the night will soon be past ;
And, if Joy has been a rover,
  'Twill return to us at last.

(*Published by* Messrs. CRAMER & Co. (Limited), *with* Mr. ALFRED COLLIER'S *Music.*)

VEGETARIAN VERSICLES.

COME, fill up your bumpers—and fill to the
    brink—
      On the present auspicious occasion ;
    Let nobody shrink from his victuals or drink,
      By an effort at artful evasion.
The fruits of the earth give our festival birth ;
  See, the apples and pears are before us !
Then, brothers, give way to unlimited mirth,
  And indulge in a limited chorus.

Chorus.

    Ev'ry scoffer that eats deleterious meats
      May at present shut up and be quiet ;
    Each epicure sees that we feast at our ease
      On a strict vegetarian diet.

Come, let us be merry. Our motto to-day
  Is, *Desipere dulce in loco.*
We all have our curds, and we all have our whey,
  And we all have our joram of cocoa.

Then pass me the grapes.   Let us banish dull care !
  Hand me over yon orange of Seville.   ·
To laugh at our banquet should any one dare,
  The intruder may go to the Old Gentleman !
                    Chorus—Ev'ry scoffer, &c.

Why slay the wild pheasant?   Why butcher the ox ?
  Or adapt the mild sheep into mutton ?
More fierce than the lions, more hard than the rocks,
  Is the gorge of the amateur glutton.
To torture dumb animals—never mind how—
  May indeed make Humanity shudder ;
The neat-handed Phillis who milketh her cow,
  Hath a heart that can feel for an udder.
                    Chorus—Ev'ry scoffer, &c.

Fight shy of the cutlet, the steak, and the chop ;
  Or I warn thee, unwary beginner,
Thine animal hankerings only may stop
  At a cut from the joint for thy dinner.
Far, far from our thoughts be the barbarous deeds
  That would hurry poor brutes to the slaughter ;
Lo ! even the lyrics we pen for our feeds
  Only savour of milk and of water.
                    Chorus—Ev'ry scoffer, &c.

MY FIRST LOVE.

E met one evening in the dance;
    When I—the greenest of Etonians—
Was fascinated by a glance
    She gave me in the "Caledonians."
The topics we enlarged upon
    Were music and the drama merely,
But soon my silly heart was gone;—
    It was indeed—or very nearly.

Long after that unguarded hour
    I sent her photographs in letters;
And did the utmost in my pow'r
    To grow as ardent as my betters.
I wooed in poetry and prose;
    In each I swore I loved her dearly.
The truth I told her, goodness knows;
    I did indeed—or very nearly.

N

An early love is quite alone ;
  It brooks no second-hand revival ;
And such a love I deemed my own
  Until I found I had a rival.
I only had myself to thank ;
  But I remember, pretty clearly,
That all my life was made a blank ;
  It was indeed—or very nearly.

And I have loved and loved again,
  And have not finished yet, it may be.
My memory can scarce retain
  That love I nursed when half a baby.
But, while I was a boy at school,
  I must confess (and quite sincerely)
I acted like a little fool ;
  I did indeed—or very nearly.

THE TWO QUESTIONS.

PINE for the hills—for the lakes—for the
    heather;
  I fervently long to be somewhere away.
    One cannot be growling all day at the weather,
  Or getting through ices and claret all day.
By Zeus, if I only could manage to borrow
  Of Cook or of Gaze a suggestion or two,
I'd pack up my traps and be off by to-morrow;—
  But where shall I wander, and what shall I do?

The squares of the West are deserted and lonely,
  The parks given o'er to estival repose;
And very few Members of Parliament only
  Will wait for the Session to crawl to its close.
I sigh for new faces, new people, and places:
  I sigh to take wing and fly off, *tout à coup*,
Too far from this hothouse to leave any traces;—
  But where shall I wander, and what shall I do?

For walking or driving, or steaming or sailing,
    I'm equally ready, as luck may decree;
And equally ready, if need be, for scaling
    The casual Alp or the chance Pyrenee.
But how can I settle my plans in a minute,
    And how can I fix upon anything new?
I pine for my journey and long to begin it ;—
    But where shall I wander, and what shall I do?

SLOWLY, BUT SURELY.

EYES where a smile very seldom, if ever is;
    Down to the ground in the deepest of reveries
        Dropt so demurely—
Speaking as little of love as of merriment,
Still you can wound, and have tried the experiment;
        Slowly, but surely.

Where there are wounds there are often recoveries,
Did you not count how forbearing a lover is
        Too prematurely?
Say to your owner, blue eyes, without fretting her,
He who adored her may end by forgetting her—
        Slowly, but surely.

"GETTING BROWNER EV'RY DAY."

I ROAMED among the meadows in October,
　　I saw the signs of winter all around.
　　The skies were growing dull and growing sober;
　　The traces of a frost were on the ground.
I saw the leaf becoming sere and yellow,
　　The giant oak beginning to decay:—
I paused awhile to murmur, "Poor old fellow;
　　Your green is getting browner ev'ry day!"

In boyhood, when my day was only early,
　　And Life worth all the gold in any mint,
My head of hair—though naturally curly—
　　Was fiercer than the carrot in its tint.
But later (by the kindly aid of dyeing)
　　It grew a lovely auburn—in its way:
And people kept perpetually crying,
　　"Young Green is getting browner ev'ry day!"

I traded on the vile dissimulation
   Until I left my own, my native land.
One morning a seductive situation
   Invited me to India's coral strand;
That climate is a test for one's complexion,
   It rendered me as dark as a Malay:
My comrades often uttered the reflection,
   "Poor Green is getting browner ev'ry day!"

One hates to be a "sham" when over fifty;
   To dye, upon my word, was *infra dig.*
And people growing old are growing thrifty;
   'Twas cheaper, on the whole, to buy a wig.
Now all my friends ironically taunt me,
   They gaze upon my flaxen head and say—
In syllables that ever seem to haunt me—
   "Why, Green, you're getting browner ev'ry day!"

MY LOUISE.

I LOVE Louise with all my might;—
　　I've breathed my love with all my main.
One fact I mention with delight ;—
　　The darling is intensely plain.
Why seek for loveliness, I pray,
　　Or charms or graces in a wife?
Deceptive Beauty flies away;
　　But Ugliness is ours for life.

Of Jealousy I've read and heard—
　　A monster with an eye of green ;
To me 'tis nothing but a *word*,
　　I know not what the *thing* may mean.
Louise is mine, my very own—
　　Of that I'm pretty well assured ;
If I've my doubts when I'm alone,
　　On seeing her my doubts are cured.

A lover fond will oft compare
  The object of his love and rhymes
With Venus or Diana fair,
  The goddesses of mythic times.
Such flatteries the present bard
  Has never penned, and never will;
For Fable I've a deep regard—
  For Truth I have a deeper still.

A DECIDED NEGATIVE.

AS a schoolboy I ever was partial to Brown.
    We divided our toffee—divided our toys
    To this minute (so schoolboys' tradition
      comes down)
We are quoted as friendly and brotherly boys.
But, supposing that Brown were to ask me to-day
    For a share of my heart or a share of my purse ;
I should sink the old friendship and stubbornly say—
    " Not at all ; on the contrary—quite the reverse."

I have known what it is to be head over heels
    In a passion that knows neither limit nor span ;
I have known what a loving young gentleman feels
    When he feels all a loving young gentleman can.
But if Laura Matilda should come to me now,
    And recall what I promised when lovesick or worse,
Do you think I should even remember my vow ?—
    No. at all ; on the contrary—quite the reverse.

I was once an implicit believer in Fame,
  And would rather have grown to be great than be
    rich;
It was all my ambition to boast of a name
  As a poet or proser (I little cared which).
I was born with a brain of my own in my head,
  And believed it a blessing, and found it a curse.
Have I now any longing to write or be read?
  Not at all; on the contrary—quite the reverse.

FROM BAD TO WORSE.

IN a part of a suburb sequestered and gloomy
    I took up my quarters a twelvemonth ago.
  My abode, I confess, was a neat one and
    roomy ;
  But—shade of Herr Zimmermann !—was it not
    slow ?
I began to resemble that owl of a Rousseau,
  Immured in a Hermitage all by myself ;
Or that insular anchorite Robinson Crusoe,
  Deserted and quietly placed on the shelf.

But the editors e'en in my solitude sought me,
  And begged for my funniments day after day ;
And the door was besieged by the postmen who
    brought me
  Requests to be comic and mention my pay.
To be comic? The captive, in fetters and lonely,
  May feed on his heart till its pulses are cold ;
To be mirthful is left for the free, and them only.
  He cannot be comic—not even for gold !

From the scene of my sadness at length I departed,
  And found a new lodging that looks on the
    Strand.
What a change! The poor cynic, of late broken-
    hearted,
  Possesses the lightest of hearts in the land.
While the crowds and the traffic float ever before
    me,
  I breathe a new life in the midst of my kind;
And the sorrows that came to my suburb to bore
    me
  No longer afflict my regenerate mind.

And the editors call at my residence daily;
  But most of them rather unfeelingly hint
That the verses I knock off so lightly and gaily
  Are scarcely sufficiently thoughtful for print.
Would I try to be touching? They're all of them
    eager
  For sentimentalities put into rhyme;—
And they think my *vis comica* grows very meagre,
  Though highly respectable once on a time.

By a plan I've invented—though not economic—
  I think I can settle the whole of the band
Who expect a suburban recluse to be comic,
  And seek to get sentiment out of the Strand.

My abode, I resolve, shall in future be double;
    One deep in a suburb, one deep in the throng.—
Then perhaps I may manage, without any trouble,
    To grasp the occasion and vary my song.

"*TWO'S COMPANY.*"

—Popular Proverb.

MISS Jenny B—— was born for me,
    And I was born for Jenny;
For any other Miss I see
    I hardly care a penny.
Two turtle-doves you never saw
    So fond of one another,
And yet my rapture hath a flaw—
    My Jenny hath a brother!

A child of eight—or under that;
    Of manners inoffensive.
You rarely find so young a brat
    With knowledge so extensive.
For him two syllables are nought
    He laughs at long-division;—
He says his lessons, as he ought,
    With laudable precision.

Due reverence for me he shows;
    He greets me as a " Mister."
The clever boy !—I know he knows
    I love his pretty sister.
It *may* be chance—and yet I see
    That more than chance is in it ;—
He never leaves Miss B—— and me
    Together for a minute.

I cannot heave the tender sigh
    With any satisfaction,
While such an incubus is by
    To mark my ev'ry action.
I cannot bend the supple knee,
    And " pop " the tender question ;
The very thought of Number Three
    Forbids the soft suggestion.

We never meet—we never talk—
    But those two eyes espy us.
We can't contrive to steal a walk
    But Number Three is nigh us.
In such a sad and sorry plight
    Perhaps it would be better
To plead my suit in black and white,
    And register the letter.

THE REJECTED.

OW smoothly runs the ballad old ;
    " Oh, say not Woman's love is bought !"
    Alas ! too often men are taught
That Woman's lover may be sold.

Those eyes were Paradises blue ;
    Their ev'ry flash a snake, designed
    To work the woe of all mankind—
As snakes in Eden ever do.

Dim thoughts of all that might have been
    Survive now Truth and Love are dead ;
    And even yet I seem to tread
On Hope's departing crinoline.

But, ere my footprint fades away,
    Despair is close upon my track ;
    And, laughing loud behind my back,
She dogs me all the dreary day.

I loved ;—I cannot love again.
 This heart is not of looking-glass—
 Reflecting pretty forms that pass ;—
Say, rather, 'tis a window-pane.

On looking through I hoped to find
 A soul responsive to my own ;
 I gaze no more—but, with a groan,
Stand pulling down the window-blind.

ON THE RACK.

I HAVE been through my alphabet carefully
    twice—
  O'er my vowels and consonants once and
    again ;
I have studied them all in a fashion precise,
  But my labour is hopeless—my efforts are vain.
Could I find the initial the rest were secure
  (For one letter would set the remainder correct) ;—
What a plague for a sensitive soul to endure
  Is a word you remember but can't recollect.

'Tis a simple machine ; you need never go far
  For a tea-bibbing circle where hostess or host
In the front of the fire has it hung from a bar,
  To retain the caloric in muffins or toast.
I have seen it in infancy—seen it in youth—
  And shall frequently see it in age, I expect.
It possesses a name—though, to tell you the truth,
  'Tis a name I remember but can't recollect.

But it is not alone in a matter like this—
  Which is hardly a matter that matters at all—
That a treacherous memory serves one amiss,
  And the things that you know you can rarely recall.
I've devoted my time to perusing the Bard
  For the purpose of quoting his verse with effect;
Yet it often occurs, when I'm not on my guard,
  That the line I remember I can't recollect.

If I go to the Opera once in a way,
  Or indulge in a Monday or Saturday " Pop,"
I am haunted, of course, through the following day
  By a tune that I cannot let utterly drop.
It is with me, though vaguely, the minute I wake;
  In the course of my shaving I stop to reflect
On a quaint modulation, a run, or a shake,
  In the air I remember but can't recollect.

I am worried and vexed from the morn till the night
  By the scraps of old memories left in my head.
I should never complain if they vanished outright,
  And the *whole* of the brief reminiscence were dead.
But my semi-revivals are bitter to bear—
  'Tis to these that I mildly but firmly object;—
Not the things that oblivion has blown into air,
  But the things I remember yet can't recollect.

LINES TO CUPID.

(OLD STYLE, VERY CURIOUS.)

WHAT, Cupid? At your thefts again
    Too bad by half, you little traitor.
    But here your efforts will be vain :
    Cantabit vacuus viator.
Yes ; point the arrow—bend the bow ;—
    At *that* your mother made you clever.
My heart's at home, Love, but I know
    There's nothing *in it* whatsoever.

You stole—but I forgive the theft—
    All that was ever worth your stealing ;
You gave it Chloe, and you left
    Nor warmth, nor sentiment, nor feeling.
I weigh my joy against my grief,
    And pardon you my fret and fever ;
For I consider Love—the *thief*—
    No worse than Chloe—the *receiver !*

MIDNIGHT MUSINGS.

IVELY prowler of the night,
    Stealthy, creeping, cruel thing ;
Say, what profit or delight
    Can thy fitful frolics bring ?
Wherefore later than the owl
Goest thou upon the prowl ?

" Now the bird is in his nest,
    While the beast is in his lair ;
Now the fishes are at rest,
    Free from sorrow, void of care.
Each and all their slumber take,
Thou alone art wide awake.

" Happy bird and happy fish ;
    Happy beast, where'er you be ;
Sleep is with you at your wish ;
    Would it were the same to *me !*
Ever watchful is my foe ;
Consequently *I* am so.

" Hence ! avaunt !   The world is wide ;
 Brighter spots may soon be found ;
Where thy prowess can be tried
 On a happier hunting-ground.
Seek thy prey across the seas,
In the wild Antipodes !

" Vex not thou the poet's brain ;
 Let him sleep and let him snore ;
Cut—but never come again ;
 Fly, farewell for evermore.
Leave me cradled in repose,
Silent, all except the nose."

Thus the bard's unsleeping lyre
 Virulently vented verse.
Reader, what aroused his ire ?
 Was it flea, or was it worse ?
Gentle reader, spare your smiles ;
'Twas a cat upon the tiles !

OH, AGONY!

JOY is a myth to me, mirth is a mockery;
    Earth is a dungeon, and life is a chain;
    Friendship and love are as brittle as crockery;
    Peace has departed and comes not again.
Long did I riot in healthful security,
    Treading on roses unmixed with a thorn;
Little I thought that my fate and futurity
    Haply might plant on my trotters a corn.

Lost are the days when my lot was a shiny one;—
    Lost from the minute I felt on my toe
Something I fancied a wart, and a tiny one,
    Mildly but firmly beginning to grow.
Never again shall I feel the tranquillity
    Born of a foot and a conscience at ease :—
Never again don a boot with facility,
    Free from a sigh and a cry and a squeeze.

Some of my friends say I ought to put oil on it :
    Others that vinegar acts as a cure.
Vainly I've wasted my time and my toil on it ;—
    Still I continue to grin and endure.
No ;—in this worst of all possible maladies
    Vinegar heals not, and oil is at fault.
Shall I at last have it drest as a salad is,
    Adding the condiments, pepper and salt?

Daily and nightly my merciless visitor
    Fills me with fury, and robs me of rest.
Never in Spain did the sternest Inquisitor
    Frame such a torture as harrows my breast.
Oft, as I limp on my day's weary wanderings,
    One of those little red-uniformed brutes
Brings to a stop my poetical ponderings
    With a suggestion of "Polish yer boots?"

P

"*A MERRY CHRISTMAS.*"

HE words are blithe and full of cheer ;
    They never pall on any hearer,
But—borne along from year to year—
    From year to year sound ever dearer.

And yet we know the words are vain ;
    We know the season *must* be merry,
When those long-severed meet again
    Below the white and scarlet berry.

When small but mirth-compelling jokes
    Are heard from every nook and corner ;—
When on the board Plum-Pudding smokes,
    Attended by the Pie of Horner.

When kissing shall by favour go,
    And Age declare it only folly
That Youth descends to mistletoe,
    And lovely Woman stoops to holly.

When old, and young, and middle-aged—
  Three generations—all commingle;
The widowed, wedded, fresh-engaged,
  And, last and least, the many single.

"Merry?"—When all around is bright?
  "Merry?"—Ay, marry; now or never.
The churl that cannot laugh to-night
  May give the habit up for ever.

One week in all the fifty-two
  Is little time to give to laughter;
Come, join the revel, cynic, *do!*
  Although a cynic ever after.

Come, choose a seasonable strain,
  To fit the jolly days before us;
And shout we all, with might and main—
  "A Merry Christmas!" is the chorus!

PRINTED BY BALLANTYNE, HANSON AND CO.
EDINBURGH AND LONDON

CHATTO & WINDUS'S
LIST OF BOOKS.

Imperial 8vo, with 147 fine Engravings, half-morocco, 36s.

THE EARLY TEUTONIC, ITALIAN,
AND FRENCH MASTERS.

Translated and Edited from the Dohme Series by A. H. KEANE, M.A.I. With numerous Illustrations.

"Cannot fail to be of the utmost use to students of art history."—TIMES.

Second Edition, Revised, Crown 8vo, 1,200 pages, half-roxburghe, 12s. 6d.

THE READER'S HANDBOOK
OF ALLUSIONS, REFERENCES, PLOTS, AND STORIES.
By the Rev. Dr. BREWER.

"*Dr. Brewer has produced a wonderfully comprehensive dictionary of references to matters which are always cropping up in conversation and in everyday life, and writers generally will have reason to feel grateful to the author for a most handy volume, supplementing in a hundred ways their own knowledge or ignorance, as the case may be. . . . It is something more than a mere dictionary of quotations, though a most useful companion to any work of that kind, being a dictionary of most of the allusions, references, plots, stories, and characters which occur in the classical poems, plays, novels, romances, &c., not only of our own country, but of most nations, ancient and modern.*"—TIMES.

"*A welcome addition to the list of what may be termed the really handy reference-books, combining as it does a dictionary of literature with a condensed encyclopædia, interspersed with items one usually looks for in commonplace books. The appendices contain the dates of celebrated and well-known dramas, operas, poems, and novels, with the names of their authors.*"—SPECTATOR.

"*Meets a want which every one, even of the thoroughly educated class, must often have felt. It would require a colossal memory indeed to dispense with Dr. Brewer's volume. . . The author of 'The Guide to Science' has gained a reputation for thoroughness . . . and a glance at 'The Reader's Handbook' will convince anyone that he has skimmed off the cream of many hundreds of volumes. . . . Such a mass of the rare and recondite was surely never before got together in a single volume.*"—GRAPHIC.

"*There seems to be scarcely anything concerning which one may not 'overhaul' Dr. Brewer's book with profit. It is a most laborious and patient compilation, and, considering the magnitude of the work, successfully performed. . . Many queries which appear in our pages could be satisfactorily answered by a reference to 'The Reader's Handbook:' no mean testimony to the value of Dr. Brewer's book.*"—NOTES AND QUERIES.

Crown 8vo, Coloured Frontispiece and Illustrations, cloth gilt, 7s. 6d.

Advertising, A History of.

From the Earliest Times. Illustrated by Anecdotes, Curious Specimens, and Notes of Successful Advertisers. By HENRY SAMPSON.

"*We have here a book to be thankful for. We recommend the present volume, which takes us through antiquity, the middle ages, and the present time, illustrating all in turn by advertisements—serious, comic, roguish, or downright rascally. The volume is full of entertainment from the first page to the last.*"—ATHENÆUM.

Crown 8vo, cloth extra, with 639 Illustrations, 7s. 6d.

Architectural Styles, A Handbook of. ·

Translated from the German of A. ROSENGARTEN by W. COLLETT-SANDARS. With 639 Illustrations.

Crown 8vo, with Portrait and Facsimile, cloth extra, 7s. 6d.

Artemus Ward's Works :

The Works of CHARLES FARRER BROWNE, better known as ARTEMUS WARD. With Portrait, Facsimile of Handwriting, &c.

Second Edition, demy 8vo, cloth extra, with Map and Illustrations, 18s.

Baker's Clouds in the East :

Travels and Adventures on the Perso-Turcoman Frontier. By VALENTINE BAKER. Second Edition, revised and corrected.

Crown 8vo, cloth extra, 6s.

Balzac.—The Comédie Humaine and its

Author. With Translations from Balzac. By H. H. WALKER.

"*Deserves the highest praise. The best compliment we can pay him is to hope that we may soon see his translation of the 'Comédie Humaine' followed by another work. Good taste, good style, and conscientious work.*"—EXAMINER.

Crown 8vo, cloth extra, 7s. 6d.

Bankers, A Handbook of London ;

With some Account of their Predecessors, the Early Goldsmiths : together with Lists of Bankers from 1677 to 1876. By F. G. HILTON PRICE.

Bardsley (Rev. C. W.), Works by :

English Surnames : Their Sources and Significations. By CHARLES WAREING BARDSLEY, M.A. Second Edition, revised throughout and considerably Enlarged. Crown 8vo, cloth extra, 7s. 6d.

"*Mr. Bardsley has faithfully consulted the original mediæval documents and works from which the origin and development of surnames can alone be satisfactorily traced. He has furnished a valuable contribution to the literature of surnames, and we hope to hear more of him in this field.*"—TIMES.

Curiosities of Puritan Nomenclature. By CHARLES W. BARDSLEY. Crown 8vo, cloth extra, 7s. 6d.

Small 4to, green and gold, 6s. 6d. ; gilt edges, 7s. 6d.

Bechstein's As Pretty as Seven,

And other German Stories. Collected by LUDWIG BECHSTEIN. Additional Tales by Brothers GRIMM, and 100 Illustrations by RICHTER.

A New Edition, crown 8vo, cloth extra, 7s. 6d.
Bartholomew Fair, Memoirs of.
By HENRY MORLEY. New Edition, with One Hundred Illustrations.

Demy 8vo, cloth extra, with Map and Illustrations, 12s.
Beerbohm's Wanderings in Patagonia;
Or, Life among the Ostrich-Hunters. By JULIUS BEERBOHM.

" Full of well-told and exciting incident. . . . . A ride, which at all times would have had a wild and savage attraction, was destined by the merest chance to prove unexpectedly perilous and adventurous. . . . . These stirring scenes, throughout which Mr. Beerbohm shows no slight degree of bravery and coolness, are described in a manner which is both spirited and modest. . . . A thoroughly readable story, which well fills up a not unmanageable volume."—GRAPHIC.

Imperial 4to, cloth extra, gilt and gilt edges, 21s. per volume.
Beautiful Pictures by British Artists:
A Gathering of Favourites from our Picture Galleries. In Two Series.

The FIRST SERIES including Examples by WILKIE, CONSTABLE, TURNER, MULREADY, LANDSEER, MACLISE, E. M. WARD, FRITH, Sir JOHN GILBERT, LESLIE, ANSDELL, MARCUS STONE, Sir NOEL PATON, FAED, EYRE CROWE, GAVIN O'NEIL, and MADOX BROWN.

The SECOND SERIES containing Pictures by ARMITAGE, FAED, GOODALL, HEMSLEY, HORSLEY, MARKS, NICHOLLS, Sir NOEL PATON, PICKERSGILL, G. SMITH, MARCUS STONE, SOLOMON, STRAIGHT, E. M. WARD, and WARREN.

All engraved on Steel in the highest style of Art. Edited, with Notices of the Artists, by SYDNEY ARMYTAGE, M.A.

" This book is well got up, and good engravings by Jeens, Lumb Stocks, and others, bring back to us Royal Academy Exhibitions of past years."—TIMES.

One Shilling Monthly, Illustrated.
Belgravia
For January contained the First Chapters of Two Novels (each to be continued throughout the year) :—I. THE CONFIDENTIAL AGENT. By JAMES PAYN, Author of " By Proxy," &c.—II. THE LEADEN CASKET. By Mrs. A. W. HUNT, Author of "Thornicroft's Model," &c. This number contained also the First of a Series of Twelve Articles on "Our Old Country Towns," with Five Illustrations by ALFRED RIMMER.

⁕ The FORTIETH Volume of BELGRAVIA, elegantly bound in crimson cloth, full gilt side and back, gilt edges, price 7s. 6d., is now ready. —Handsome Cases for binding volumes can be had at 2s. each.

Demy 8vo, Illustrated, uniform in size for binding.
Blackburn's Art Handbooks:
Academy Notes, 1875. With 40 Illustrations. 1s.
Academy Notes, 1876. With 107 Illustrations. 1s.
Academy Notes, 1877. With 143 Illustrations. 1s.
Academy Notes, 1878. With 150 Illustrations. 1s.
Academy Notes, 1879. With 146 Illustrations. 1s.
Academy Notes, 1880. With Numerous Illustrations. [Shortly.
Grosvenor Notes, 1878. With 68 Illustrations. 1s.

ART HANDBOOKS—*continued.*
  Grosvenor Notes, 1879. With 60 Illustrations. 1*s.*
  Grosvenor Notes, 1880. With Numerous Illusts. [*Shortly.*
  Pictures at the Paris Exhibition, 1878. 80 Illustrations. 1*s.*
  Pictures at South Kensington. (The Raphael Cartoons, Sheep-
    shanks Collection, &c.) With 70 Illustrations. 1*s.*
  The English Pictures at the National Gallery. With 114
    Illustrations. 1*s.*
  The Old Masters at the National Gallery. 128 Illusts. 1*s.* 6*d.*
  Academy Notes, 1875-79. Complete in One Volume, with
    nearly 600 Illustrations in Facsimile. Demy 8vo, cloth limp, 6*s.*
  A Complete Illustrated Catalogue to the National Gallery.
    With Notes by HENRY BLACKBURN, and 242 Illustrations. Demy 8vo,
    cloth limp, 3*s.*

      UNIFORM WITH "ACADEMY NOTES."
  Royal Scottish Academy Notes, 1878. 117 Illustrations. 1*s.*
  Royal Scottish Academy Notes, 1879. 125 Illustrations. 1*s.*
  Glasgow Institute of Fine Arts Notes, 1878. 95 Illustrations. 1*s.*
  Glasgow Institute of Fine Arts Notes, 1879. 100 Illusts. 1*s.*
  Walker Art Gallery Notes, Liverpool, 1878. 112 Illusts. 1*s.*
  Walker Art Gallery Notes, Liverpool, 1879. 100 Illusts. 1*s.*
  Royal Manchester Institution Notes, 1878. 88 Illustrations. 1*s.*
  Society of Artists Notes, Birmingham, 1878. 95 Illusts. 1*s.*
  Children of the Great City. By F. W. LAWSON. With Fac-
    simile Sketches by the Artist. Demy 8vo, 1*s.*

        Folio, half-bound boards, India Proofs, 21*s.*

Blake (William) :
  Etchings from his Works. By W. B. SCOTT. With descriptive Text.
  " The best side of Blake's work is given here, and makes a really attractive
  volume, which all can enjoy. . . . The etching is of the best kind, more refined
  and delicate than the original work."—SATURDAY REVIEW.

      Crown 8vo, cloth extra, gilt, with Illustrations, 7*s.* 6*d.*

Boccaccio's Decameron ;
  or, Ten Days' Entertainment. Translated into English, with an Introduction by THOMAS WRIGHT, Esq., M.A., F.S.A. With Portrait, and
  STOTHARD'S beautiful Copperplates.

        Crown 8vo, cloth extra, gilt, 7*s.* 6*d.*

Brand's Observations on Popular Antiquities,
  chiefly Illustrating the Origin of our Vulgar Customs, Ceremonies, and
  Superstitions. With the Additions of Sir HENRY ELLIS. An entirely
  New and Revised Edition, with fine full-page Illustrations.

Bowers' (Georgina) Hunting Sketches :
  Canters in Crampshire. By G. BOWERS. I. Gallops from
    Gorseborough. II. Scrambles with Scratch Packs. III. Studies with
    Stag Hounds. Oblong 4to, half-bound boards, 21*s.*
  Leaves from a Hunting Journal. By G. BOWERS. Coloured in
    facsimile of the originals. Oblong 4to, half-bound, 21*s.* [*Nearly Ready.*

Bret Harte, Works by:

The Select Works of Bret Harte, in Prose and Poetry. With Introductory Essay by J. M. BELLEW, Portrait of the Author, and 50 Illustrations. Crown 8vo, cloth extra, 7s. 6d.

An Heiress of Red Dog, and other Stories. By BRET HARTE. Post 8vo, illustrated boards, 2s.; cloth limp, 2s. 6d.

"Few modern English-writing humourists have achieved the popularity of Mr. Bret Harte. He has passed, so to speak, beyond book-fame into talk-fame. People who may never perhaps have held one of his little volumes in their hands, are perfectly familiar with some at least of their contents . . . . Pictures of Californian camp-life, unapproached in their quaint picturesqueness and deep human interest."—DAILY NEWS.

The Twins of Table Mountain. By BRET HARTE. Fcap. 8vo, picture cover, 1s.; crown 8vo, cloth extra, 3s. 6d.

The Luck of Roaring Camp, and other Sketches. By BRET HARTE. Post 8vo, illustrated boards, 2s.

Jeff Briggs's Love Story. By BRET HARTE. Fcap. 8vo, picture cover, 1s.; cloth extra, 2s. 6d.

Small crown 8vo, cloth extra, gilt, with full-page Portraits, 4s. 6d.

Brewster's (Sir David) Martyrs of Science.

Small crown 8vo, cloth extra, gilt, with Astronomical Plates, 4s. 6d.

Brewster's (Sir D.) More Worlds than One,

the Creed of the Philosopher and the Hope of the Christian.

Demy 8vo, profusely Illustrated in Colours, 30s.

British Flora Medica:

A History of the Medicinal Plants of Great Britain. Illustrated by a Figure of each Plant, COLOURED BY HAND. By BENJAMIN H. BARTON, F.L.S., and THOMAS CASTLE, M.D., F.R.S. A New Edition, revised and partly re-written by JOHN R. JACKSON, A.L.S., Curator of the Museums of Economic Botany, Royal Gardens, Kew.

THE STOTHARD BUNYAN.—Crown 8vo, cloth extra, gilt, 7s. 6d.

Bunyan's Pilgrim's Progress.

Edited by Rev. T. SCOTT. With 17 beautiful Steel Plates by STOTHARD, engraved by GOODALL; and numerous Woodcuts.

Crown 8vo, cloth extra, gilt, with Illustrations, 7s. 6d.

Byron's Letters and Journals.

With Notices of his Life. By THOMAS MOORE. A Reprint of the Original Edition newly revised, with Twelve full-page Plates.

Demy 8vo, cloth extra, 14s.

Campbell's (Sir G.) White and Black:

The Outcome of a Visit to the United States. By Sir GEORGE CAMPBELL, M.P.

"Few persons are likely to take it up without finishing it."—NONCONFORMIST.

Crown 8vo, cloth extra, 1s. 6d.

Carlyle (Thomas) On the Choice of Books.
With Portrait and Memoir.

Small 4to, cloth gilt, with Coloured Illustrations, 10s. 6d.

Chaucer for Children:
A Golden Key. By Mrs. H. R. HAWEIS. With Eight Coloured
Pictures and numerous Woodcuts by the Author.

"*It must not only take a high place among the Christmas and New Year books
of this season, but is also of permanent value as an introduction to the study of
Chaucer, whose works, in selections of some kind or other, are now text-books in
every school that aspires to give sound instruction in English.*"—ACADEMY.

Crown 8vo, cloth limp, with Map and Illustrations, 2s. 6d.

Cleopatra's Needle:
Its Acquisition and Removal to England Described. By Sir J. E.
ALEXANDER.

Crown 8vo, cloth extra, gilt, 7s. 6d.

Colman's Humorous Works:
"Broad Grins," "My Nightgown and Slippers," and other Humorous
Works, Prose and Poetical, of GEORGE COLMAN. With Life by G.
B. BUCKSTONE, and Frontispiece by HOGARTH.

Two Vols. royal 8vo, with Sixty-five Illustrations, 28s.

Conway's Demonology and Devil-Lore.
By MONCURE DANIEL CONWAY, M.A., B.D. of Divinity College,
Harvard University; Member of the Anthropological Inst., London.

Square 8vo, cloth extra, profusely Illustrated, 6s.

Conway's A Necklace of Stories.
By MONCURE D. CONWAY. Illustrated by W. J. HENNESSY.

Demy 8vo, cloth extra, with Coloured Illustrations and Maps, 24s.

Cope's History of the Rifle Brigade
(The Prince Consort's Own), formerly the 95th. By Sir WILLIAM
H. COPE, formerly Lieutenant, Rifle Brigade.

Crown 8vo, cloth extra, gilt, with 13 Portraits, 7s. 6d.

Creasy's Memoirs of Eminent Etonians;
with Notices of the Early History of Eton College. By Sir EDWARD
CREASY, Author of "The Fifteen Decisive Battles of the World."

"*A new edition of 'Creasy's Etonians' will be welcome. The book was a
favourite a quarter of a century ago, and it has maintained its reputation. The
value of this new edition is enhanced by the fact that Sir Edward Creasy has
added to it several memoirs of Etonians who have died since the first edition
prepared. The work is eminently interesting.*"—SCOTSMAN.

Crown 8vo, cloth extra, with Frontispiece, 7s. 6d.

Credulities, Past and Present.
By WILLIAM JONES, F.S.A., Author of "Finger-Ring Lore," &c.
[*In the Press.*

Crown 8vo, cloth gilt, Two very thick Volumes, 7s. 6d. each.

Cruikshank's Comic Almanack.

Complete in TWO SERIES: The FIRST from 1835 to 1843 ; the SECOND from 1844 to 1853. A Gathering of the BEST HUMOUR of THACKERAY, HOOD, MAYHEW, ALBERT SMITH, A'BECKETT, ROBERT BROUGH, &c. With 2,000 Woodcuts and Steel Engravings by CRUIKSHANK, HINE, LANDELLS, &c.

Parts I. to XIV. now ready, 21s. each.

Cussans' History of Hertfordshire.

By JOHN E. CUSSANS. Illustrated with full-page Plates on Copper and Stone, and a profusion of small Woodcuts.

" Mr. Cussans has, from sources not accessible to Clutterbuck, made most valuable additions to the manorial history of the county from the earliest period downwards, cleared up many doubtful points, and given original details concerning various subjects untouched or imperfectly treated by that writer. The pedigrees seem to have been constructed with great care, and are a valuable addition to the genealogical history of the county. Mr. Cussans appears to have done his work conscientiously, and to have spared neither time, labour, nor expense to render his volumes worthy of ranking in the highest class of County Histories." —ACADEMY.

Two Volumes, demy 4to, handsomely bound in half-morocco, gilt, profusely Illustrated with Coloured and Plain Plates and Woodcuts, price £7 7s.

Cyclopædia of Costume;

or, A Dictionary of Dress—Regal, Ecclesiastical, Civil, and Military— from the Earliest Period in England to the reign of George the Third. Including Notices of Contemporaneous Fashions on the Continent, and a General History of the Costumes of the Principal Countries of Europe. By J. R. PLANCHÉ, Somerset Herald.

The Volumes may also be had *separately* (each Complete in itself) at £3 13s.6d. each:

Vol. I. THE DICTIONARY.

Vol. II. A GENERAL HISTORY OF COSTUME IN EUROPE.

Also in 25 Parts, at 5s. each. Cases for binding, 5s. each.

" A comprehensive and highly valuable book of reference. . . . We have rarely failed to find in this book an account of an article of dress, while in most of the entries curious and instructive details are given. . . . Mr. Planché's enormous labour of love, the production of a text which, whether in its dictionary form or in that of the 'General History,' is within its intended scope immeasurably the best and richest work on Costume in English. . . . This book is not only one of the most readable works of the kind, but intrinsically attractive and amusing."—ATHENÆUM.

" A most readable and interesting work—and it can scarcely be consulted in vain, whether the reader is in search for information as to military, court, ecclesiastical, legal, or professional costume. . . . All the chromo-lithographs, and most of the woodcut illustrations—the latter amounting to several thousands —are very elaborately executed; and the work forms a livre de luxe which renders it equally suited to the library and the ladies' drawing-room."—TIMES.

" One of the most perfect works ever published upon the subject. The illustrations are numerous and excellent, and would, even without the letterpress, render the work an invaluable book of reference for information as to costumes for fancy balls and character quadrilles. . . . Beautifully printed and superbly illustrated."—STANDARD.

Second Edition, revised and enlarged, demy 8vo, cloth extra,
with Illustrations, 24s.

Dodge's (Colonel) The Hunting Grounds of

the Great West : A Description of the Plains, Game, and Indians of
the Great North American Desert.   By RICHARD IRVING DODGE,
Lieutenant-Colonel of the United States Army.   With an Introduction
by WILLIAM BLACKMORE ; Map, and numerous Illustrations drawn
by ERNEST GRISET.

"*This magnificent volume is one of the most able and most interesting works
which has ever proceeded from an American pen, while its freshness is equal to
that of any similar book.   Col. Dodge has chosen a subject of which he is master,
and treated it with a fulness that leaves nothing to be desired, and in a style which
is charming equally for its picturesqueness and purity.*"—NONCONFORMIST.

Demy 8vo, cloth extra, 12s. 6d.

Doran's Memories of our Great Towns.

With Anecdotic Gleanings concerning their Worthies and their
Oddities.   By Dr. JOHN DORAN, F.S.A.

"*A greater genius for writing of the anecdotic kind few men have had.   As
to giving any idea of the contents of the book, it is quite impossible.   Those who
know how Dr. Doran used to write—it is sad to have to use the past tense of one of
the most cheerful of men—will understand what we mean ; and those who do not
must take it on trust from us that this is a remarkably entertaining volume.*"—
SPECTATOR.

Second Edition, demy 8vo, cloth gilt, with Illustrations, 18s.

Dunraven's The Great Divide :

A Narrative of Travels in the Upper Yellowstone in the Summer of
1874.   By the EARL of DUNRAVEN.   With Maps and numerous
striking full-page Illustrations by VALENTINE W. BROMLEY.

"*There has not for a long time appeared a better book of travel than Lord
Dunraven's 'The Great Divide.'   . . .   The book is full of clever observation,
and both narrative and illustrations are thoroughly good.*"—ATHENÆUM.

Demy 8vo, cloth, 16s.

Dutt's India, Past and Present;

with Minor Essays on Cognate Subjects.   By SHOSHEE CHUNDER
DUTT, Rái Báhádoor.

Crown 8vo, cloth extra, gilt, with Illustrations, 6s.

Emanuel On Diamonds and Precious

Stones ; their History, Value, and Properties ; with Simple Tests for
ascertaining their Reality.   By HARRY EMANUEL, F.R.G.S.   With
numerous Illustrations, Tinted and Plain.

Crown 8vo, cloth extra, with Illustrations, 7s. 6d.

Englishman's House, The :

A Practical Guide to all interested in Selecting or Building a House,
with full Estimates of Cost, Quantities, &c.   By C. J. RICHARDSON.
Third Edition.   With nearly 600 Illustrations.

Crown 8vo, cloth boards, 6s. per Volume.

Early English Poets.

Edited, with Introductions and Annotations, by Rev. A. B. GROSART.

"*Mr. Grosart has spent the most laborious and the most enthusiastic care on the perfect restoration and preservation of the text; and it is very unlikely that any other edition of the poet can ever be called for. . . From Mr. Grosart we always expect and always receive the final results of most patient and competent scholarship.*"—EXAMINER.

1. **Fletcher's (Giles, B.D.) Complete Poems:** Christ's Victorie in Heaven, Christ's Victorie on Earth, Christ's Triumph over Death, and Minor Poems. With Memorial-Introduction and Notes. One Vol.

2. **Davies' (Sir John) Complete Poetical Works,** including Psalms I. to L. in Verse, and other hitherto Unpublished MSS., for the first time Collected and Edited. Memorial-Introduction and Notes. Two Vols.

3. **Herrick's (Robert) Hesperides, Noble Numbers, and Complete Collected Poems.** With Memorial-Introduction and Notes, Steel Portrait, Index of First Lines, and Glossarial Index, &c. Three Vols.

4. **Sidney's (Sir Philip) Complete Poetical Works,** including all those in "Arcadia." With Portrait, Memorial-Introduction, Essay on the Poetry of Sidney, and Notes. Three Vols.

Folio, cloth extra, £1 11s. 6d.

Examples of Contemporary Art.

Etchings from Representative Works by living English and Foreign Artists. Edited, with Critical Notes, by J. COMYNS CARR.

"*It would not be easy to meet with a more sumptuous, and at the same time a more tasteful and instructive drawing-room book.*"—NONCONFORMIST.

Crown 8vo, cloth extra, with Illustrations, 6s.

Fairholt's Tobacco :

Its History and Associations; with an Account of the Plant and its Manufacture, and its Modes of Use in all Ages and Countries. By F. W. FAIRHOLT, F.S.A. With Coloured Frontispiece and upwards of 100 Illustrations by the Author.

"*A very pleasant and instructive his'ory of tobacco and its associations, which we cordially recommend alike to the votaries and to the enemies of the much-maligned but certainly not neglected weed. . . . Full of interest and information.*"—DAILY NEWS.

Crown 8vo, cloth extra, with Illustrations, 4s. 6d.

Faraday's Chemical History of a Candle.

Lectures delivered to a Juvenile Audience. A New Edition. Edited by W. CROOKES, F.C.S. With numerous Illustrations.

Crown 8vo, cloth extra, with Illustrations, 4s. 6d.

Faraday's Various Forces of Nature.

New Edition. Edited by W. CROOKES, F.C.S. Numerous Illustrations.

Crown 8vo, cloth extra, with Illustrations, 7s. 6d.

Finger-Ring Lore :

Historical, Legendary, and Anecdotal. By WM. JONES, F.S.A. With Hundreds of Illustrations of Curious Rings of all Ages and Countries.

"*One of those gossiping books which are as full of amusement as of instruction.*"—ATHENÆUM.

One Shilling Monthly, mostly Illustrated.

Gentleman's Magazine, The,

For January contained the First Chapters of a New Novel entitled
QUEEN COPHETUA, by R. E. FRANCILLON : to be continued throughout the year.

*** *Now ready, the Volume for* JULY *to* DECEMBER, 1879, *cloth extra,
price* 8s. 6d.; *and Cases for binding, price* 2s. *each.*

THE RUSKIN GRIMM.—Square 8vo, cloth extra, 6s. 6d. ;
gilt edges, 7s. 6d.

German Popular Stories.

Collected by the Brothers GRIMM, and Translated by EDGAR TAYLOR.
Edited with an Introduction by JOHN RUSKIN. With 22 Illustrations
after the inimitable designs of GEORGE CRUIKSHANK. Both Series
Complete.

" *The illustrations of this volume . . . are of quite sterling and admirable
art, of a class precisely parallel in elevation to the character of the tales which
they illustrate; and the original etchings, as I have before said in the Appendix to
my 'Elements of Drawing,' were unrivalled in masterfulness of touch since Rembrandt (in some qualities of delineation, unrivalled even by him). . . . To make
somewhat enlarged copies of them, looking at them through a magnifying glass,
and never putting two lines where Cruikshank has put only one, would be an exercise in decision and severe drawing which would leave afterwards little to be learnt
in schools.*"—*Extract from Introduction by* JOHN RUSKIN.

Post 8vo, cloth limp, 2s. 6d.

Glenny's A Year's Work in Garden and

Greenhouse : Practical Advice to Amateur Gardeners as to the
Management of the Flower, Fruit, and Frame Garden. By GEORGE
GLENNY.

" *Mr. Glenny has given a great deal of valuable information, conveyed in very
simple language. The amateur need not wish for a better guide.*"—LEEDS MER
CURY.

A thoroughly practical and useful handbook."—GRAPHIC.

A New Edition, demy 8vo, cloth extra, with Illustrations, 15s.

Greeks and Romans, The Life of the,

Described from Antique Monuments. By ERNST GUHL and W.
KONER. Translated from the Third German Edition, and Edited by
Dr. F. HUEFFER. With 545 Illustrations.

Crown 8vo, cloth extra, gilt, with Illustrations, 7s. 6d.

Greenwood's Low-Life Deeps :

An Account of the Strange Fish to be found there. By JAMES GREEN
WOOD. With Illustrations in tint by ALFRED CONCANEN.

Crown 8vo, cloth extra, gilt, with Illustrations, 7s. 6d.

Greenwood's Wilds of London :

Descriptive Sketches, from Personal Observations and Experience, of
Remarkable Scenes, People, and Places in London. By JAMES GREEN
WOOD. With 12 Tinted Illustrations by ALFRED CONCANEN.

Square 16mo (Tauchnitz size), cloth extra, 2s. per volume.

Golden Library, The:

Ballad History of England. By W. C. BENNETT.

Bayard Taylor's Diversions of the Echo Club.

Byron's Don Juan.

Emerson's Letters and Social Aims.

Godwin's (William) Lives of the Necromancers.

Holmes's Autocrat of the Breakfast Table. With an Introduction by G. A. SALA.

Holmes's Professor at the Breakfast Table.

Hood's Whims and Oddities. Complete. With all the original Illustrations.

Irving's (Washington) Tales of a Traveller.

Irving's (Washington) Tales of the Alhambra.

Jesse's (Edward) Scenes and Occupations of Country Life.

Lamb's Essays of Elia. Both Series Complete in One Vol.

Leigh Hunt's Essays: A Tale for a Chimney Corner, and other Pieces. With Portrait, and Introduction by EDMUND OLLIER.

Mallory's (Sir Thomas) Mort d'Arthur: The Stories of King Arthur and of the Knights of the Round Table. Edited by B. MONTGOMERIE RANKING.

Pascal's Provincial Letters. A New Translation, with Historical Introduction and Notes, by T. M'CRIE, D.D.

Pope's Poetical Works. Complete.

Rochefoucauld's Maxims and Moral Reflections. With Notes, and an Introductory Essay by SAINTE-BEUVE.

St. Pierre's Paul and Virginia, and The Indian Cottage. Edited, with Life, by the Rev. E. CLARKE.

Shelley's Early Poems, and Queen Mab, with Essay by LEIGH HUNT.

Shelley's Later Poems: Laon and Cythna, &c.

Shelley's Posthumous Poems, the Shelley Papers, &c.

Shelley's Prose Works, including A Refutation of Deism, Zastrozzi, St. Irvyne, &c.

White's Natural History of Selborne. Edited, with additions, by THOMAS BROWN, F.L.S.

Crown 8vo, cloth gilt and gilt edges, 7s. 6d.

Golden Treasury of Thought, The:

An ENCYCLOPÆDIA OF QUOTATIONS from Writers of all Times and Countries. Selected and Edited by THEODORE TAYLOR.

Large 4to, with 14 facsimile Plates, price ONE GUINEA.

Grosvenor Gallery Illustrated Catalogue.

Winter Exhibition (1877–78) of Drawings by the Old Masters and Water-Colour Drawings by Deceased Artists of the British School. With a Critical Introduction by J. COMYNS CARR.

Crown 8vo, cloth extra, gilt, with Illustrations, 4s. 6d.

Guyot's Earth and Man;

or, Physical Geography in its Relation to the History of Mankind. With Additions by Professors AGASSIZ, PIERCE, and GRAY; 12 Maps and Engravings on Steel, some Coloured, and copious Index.

Small 4to, cloth extra, 8*s*.

Hake's Maiden Ecstasy.

By THOMAS GORDON HAKE, Author of " Parables and Tales,"
"New Symbols," " Legends of the Morrow," &c.

Medium 8vo, cloth extra, gilt, with Illustrations, 7*s*. 6*d*.

Hall's (Mrs. S. C.) Sketches of Irish Character.

With numerous Illustrations on Steel and Wood by MACLISE, GIL-
BERT, HARVEY, and G. CRUIKSHANK.

*"The Irish Sketches of this lady resemble Miss Mitford's beautiful English
sketches in ' Our Village,' but they are far more vigorous and picturesque and
bright."*—BLACKWOOD'S MAGAZINE.

Post 8vo, cloth extra, 4*s*. 6*d*.; a few large-paper copies, half-Roxb., 10*s*. 6*d*.

Handwriting, The Philosophy of.

By Don FELIX DE SALAMANCA.   With 134 Facsimiles of Signatures.

Haweis (Mrs.), Works by :

The Art of Dress. By Mrs. H. R. HAWEIS, Author of " The
Art of Beauty," &c. Illustrated by the Author. Small 8vo, illustrated
cover, 1*s*. ; cloth limp, 1*s*. 6*d*.

*" A well-considered attempt to apply canons of good taste to the costumes
of ladies of our time. . . . . Mrs. Haweis writes frankly and to the
point, she does not mince matters, but boldly remonstrates with her own sex
on the follies they indulge in. . . . . We may recommend the book to the
ladies whom it concerns."*—ATHENÆUM.

The Art of Beauty. By Mrs. H. R. HAWEIS, Author of
" Chaucer for Children." Square 8vo, cloth extra, gilt, gilt edges, with
Coloured Frontispiece and nearly 100 Illustrations, 10*s*. 6*d*.

Vols. I. and II., demy 8vo, 12*s*. each.

History of Our Own Times, from the Accession
of Queen Victoria to the Berlin Congress. By JUSTIN MCCARTHY.

*" Criticism is disarmed before a composition which provokes little but approval.
This is a really good book on a really interesting subject, and words piled on words
could say no more for it. . . . Such is the effect of its general justice, its breadth
of view, and its sparkling buoyancy, that very few of its readers will close these
volumes without looking forward with interest to the two that are to follow."*—
SATURDAY REVIEW.

** Vols. III. and IV., completing the work, will be ready immediately.

Crown 8vo, cloth extra, 5*s*.

Hobhouse's The Dead Hand :

Addresses on the subject of Endowments and Settlements of Property.
By Sir ARTHUR HOBHOUSE, Q.C., K.C.S.I.

Crown 8vo, cloth limp, with Illustrations, 2*s*. 6*d*.

Holmes's The Science of Voice Production

and Voice Preservation : A Popular Manual for the Use of Speakers
and Singers. By GORDON HOLMES, L.R.C.P.E.

Crown 8vo, cloth extra, 4s. 6d.

Hollingshead's (John) Plain English.

[*In the press.*

Crown 8vo, cloth extra, gilt, 7s. 6d.

Hood's (Thomas) Choice Works,

In Prose and Verse. Including the CREAM OF THE COMIC ANNUALS. With Life of the Author, Portrait, and Two Hundred Illustrations.

Square crown 8vo, cloth extra, gilt edges, 6s.

Hood's (Tom) From Nowhere to the North

Pole : A Noah's Arkæological Narrative. With 25 Illustrations by W. BRUNTON and E. C. BARNES.

"*The amusing letterpress is profusely interspersed with the jingling rhymes which children love and learn so easily. Messrs. Brunton and Barnes do full justice to the writer's meaning, and a pleasanter result of the harmonious co-operation of author and artist could not be desired.*"—TIMES.

Crown 8vo, cloth extra, gilt, 7s. 6d.

Hook's (Theodore) Choice Humorous Works,

including his Ludicrous Adventures, Bons-mots, Puns, and Hoaxes. With a new Life of the Author, Portraits, Facsimiles, and Illustrations.

Crown 8vo, cloth extra, 7s.

Horne's Orion:

An Epic Poem in Three Books. By RICHARD HENGIST HORNE. With a brief Commentary by the Author. With Photographic Portrait from a Medallion by SUMMERS. Tenth Edition.

"*As classic in its own way as Keats's ' Endymion,' teeming with a Shakespearean wealth of imagery, full of clear-cut scenes from nature, and idealised with lofty thoughts.*"—WESTMINSTER REVIEW.

Crown 8vo, cloth extra, 7s. 6d.

Howell's Conflicts of Capital and Labour

Historically and Economically considered. Being a History and Review of the Trade Unions of Great Britain, showing their Origin, Progress, Constitution, and Objects, in their Political, Social, Economical, and Industrial Aspects. By GEORGE HOWELL.

"*This book is an attempt, and on the whole a successful attempt, to place the work of trade unions in the past, and their objects in the future, fairly before the public from the working man's point of view.*"—PALL MALL GAZETTE.

Demy 8vo, cloth extra, 12s. 6d.

Hueffer's The Troubadours:

A History of Provencal Life and Literature in the Middle Ages. By FRANCIS HUEFFER.

Two Vols. 8vo, with 52 Illustrations and Maps, cloth extra, gilt, 14s.

Josephus, The Complete Works of.

Translated by WHISTON. Containing both "The Antiquities of the Jews" and "The Wars of the Jews."

A NEW EDITION, Revised and partly Re-written, with several New Chapters and Illustrations, crown 8vo, cloth extra, 7s. 6d.

Jennings' The Rosicrucians:

Their Rites and Mysteries. With Chapters on the Ancient Fire and Serpent Worshippers. By HARGRAVE JENNINGS. With Five full-page Plates and upwards of 300 Illustrations.

"*One of those volumes which may be taken up and dipped into at random for half-an-hour's reading, or, on the other hand, appealed to by the student as a source of valuable information on a system which has not only exercised for hundreds of years an extraordinary influence on the mental development of so shrewd a people as the Jews, but has captivated the minds of some of the greatest thinkers of Christendom in the sixteenth and seventeenth centuries.*"—LEEDS MERCURY.

Small 8vo, cloth, full gilt, gilt edges, with Illustrations, 6s.

Kavanaghs' Pearl Fountain,

And other Fairy Stories. By BRIDGET and JULIA KAVANAGH. With Thirty Illustrations by J. MOYR SMITH.

"*Genuine new fairy stories of the old type, some of them as delightful as the best of Grimm's 'German Popular Stories.' . . . . For the most part the stories are downright, thorough-going fairy stories of the most admirable kind. . . . Mr. Moyr Smith's illustrations, too, are admirable.*"—SPECTATOR.

Crown 8vo, illustrated boards, with numerous Plates, 2s. 6d.

Lace (Old Point), and How to Copy and

Imitate it. By DAISY WATERHOUSE HAWKINS. With 17 Illustrations by the Author.

Crown 8vo, cloth extra, with numerous Illustrations, 10s. 6d.

Lamb (Mary and Charles):

Their Poems, Letters, and Remains. With Reminiscences and Notes by W. CAREW HAZLITT. With HANCOCK's Portrait of the Essayist, Facsimiles of the Title-pages of the rare First Editions of Lamb's and Coleridge's Works, and numerous Illustrations.

"*Very many passages will delight those fond of literary trifles; hardly any portion will fail in interest for lovers of Charles Lamb and his sister.*"—STANDARD.

Small 8vo, cloth extra, 5s.

Lamb's Poetry for Children, and Prince

Dorus. Carefully Reprinted from unique copies.

"*The quaint and delightful little book, over the recovery of which all the hearts of his lovers are yet warm with rejoicing.*"—A. C. SWINBURNE.

Crown 8vo, cloth extra, gilt, with Portraits, 7s. 6d.

Lamb's Complete Works,

In Prose and Verse, reprinted from the Original Editions, with many Pieces hitherto unpublished. Edited, with Notes and Introduction, by R. H. SHEPHERD. With Two Portraits and Facsimile of a Page of the "Essay on Roast Pig."

"*A complete edition of Lamb's writings, in prose and verse, has long been wanted, and is now supplied. The editor appears to have taken great pains to bring together Lamb's scattered contributions, and his collection contains a number of pieces which are now reproduced for the first time since their original appearance in various old periodicals.*"—SATURDAY REVIEW.

Demy 8vo, cloth extra, with Maps and Illustrations, 18*s.*

Lamont's Yachting in the Arctic Seas;

or, Notes of Five Voyages of Sport and Discovery in the Neighbourhood of Spitzbergen and Novaya Zemlya. By JAMES LAMONT, F.R.G.S. With numerous full-page Illustrations by Dr. LIVESAY.

"After wading through numberless volumes of icy fiction, concocted narrative, and spurious biography of Arctic voyagers, it is pleasant to meet with a real and genuine volume. . . . He shows much tact in recounting his adventures, and they are so interspersed with anecdotes and information as to make them anything but wearisome. . . . The book, as a whole, is the most important addition made to our Arctic literature for a long time."—ATHENÆUM.

Crown 8vo, cloth, full gilt, 7*s.* 6*d.*

Latter-Day Lyrics:

Poems of Sentiment and Reflection by Living Writers; selected and arranged, with Notes, by W. DAVENPORT ADAMS. With a Note on some Foreign Forms of Verse, by AUSTIN DOBSON.

Crown 8vo, cloth, full gilt, 6*s.*

Leigh's A Town Garland.

By HENRY S. LEIGH, Author of "Carols of Cockayne."

"If Mr. Leigh's verse survive to a future generation—and there is no reason why that honour should not be accorded productions so delicate, so finished, and so full of humour—their author will probably be remembered as the Poet of the Strand. . . . . Very whimsically does Mr. Leigh treat the subjects which commend themselves to him. His verse is always admirable in rhythm, and his rhymes are happy enough to deserve a place by the best of Barham. . . . . The entire contents of the volume are equally noteworthy for humour and for daintiness of workmanship."—ATHENÆUM.

SECOND EDITION.—Crown 8vo, cloth extra, with Illustrations, 10*s.* 6*d.*

Leisure-Time Studies, chiefly Biological.

By ANDREW WILSON, Ph.D., Lecturer on Zoology and Comparative Anatomy in the Edinburgh Medical School.

"It is well when we can take up the work of a really qualified investigator, who in the intervals of his more serious professional labours sets himself to impart knowledge in such a simple and elementary form as may attract and instruct, with no danger of misleading the tyro in natural science. Such a work is this little volume, made up of essays and addresses written and delivered by Dr. Andrew Wilson, lecturer and examiner in science at Edinburgh and Glasgow, at leisure intervals in a busy professional life. . . . Dr. Wilson's pages teem with matter stimulating to a healthy love of science and a reverence for the truths of nature."—SATURDAY REVIEW.

Crown 8vo, cloth extra, with Illustrations, 7*s.* 6*d.*

Life in London;

or, The History of Jerry Hawthorn and Corinthian Tom. With the whole of CRUIKSHANK'S Illustrations, in Colours, after the Originals.

Crown 8vo, cloth extra, 6*s.*

Lights on the Way:

Some Tales within a Tale. By the late J. H. ALEXANDER, B.A. Edited, with an Explanatory Note, by H. A. PAGE, Author of "Thoreau: A Study."

Crown 8vo, cloth extra, with Illustrations, 7s. 6d.

Longfellow's Complete Prose Works.

Including "Outre Mer," "Hyperion," "Kavanagh," "The Poets and Poetry of Europe," and "Driftwood." With Portrait and Illustrations by VALENTINE BROMLEY.

Crown 8vo, cloth extra, gilt, with Illustrations, 7s. 6d.

Longfellow's Poetical Works.

Carefully Reprinted from the Original Editions. With numerous fine Illustrations on Steel and Wood.

Crown 8vo, cloth extra, 5s.

Lunatic Asylum, My Experiences in a.

By a SANE PATIENT.

"*The story is clever and interesting, sad beyond measure though the subject be. There is no personal bitterness, and no violence or anger. Whatever may have been the evidence for our author's madness when he was consigned to an asylum, nothing can be clearer than his sanity when he wrote this book; it is bright, calm, and to the point.*"—SPECTATOR.

Demy 8vo, with Fourteen full-page Plates, cloth boards, 18s.

Lusiad (The) of Camoens.

Translated into English Spenserian verse by ROBERT FFRENCH DUFF, Knight Commander of the Portuguese Royal Order of Christ.

Macquoid (Mrs.), Works by:

Pictures and Legends from Normandy and Brittany. By KATHARINE S. MACQUOID. With numerous Illustrations by THOMAS R. MACQUOID. Square 8vo, cloth gilt, 10s. 6d.

"*Mr. and Mrs. Macquoid have been strolling in Normandy and Brittany, and the result of their observations and researches in that picturesque land of romantic associations is an attractive volume, which is neither a work of travel nor a collection of stories, but a book partaking almost in equal degree of each of these characters. . . . The illustrations, which are numerous, are drawn, as a rule, with remarkable delicacy as well as with true artistic feeling.*"—DAILY NEWS.

Through Normandy. By KATHARINE S. MACQUOID. With 90 Illustrations by T. R. MACQUOID. Square 8vo, cloth extra, 7s. 6d.

"*The illustrations are excellent, and the work is pleasant as well as accurate.*"—ATHENÆUM.
"*One of the few books which can be read as a piece of literature, whilst at the same time handy and serviceable in the knapsack.*"—BRITISH QUARTERLY REVIEW.

Through Brittany. By KATHARINE S. MACQUOID. With numerous Illustrations by THOMAS R. MACQUOID. Square 8vo, cloth extra, 7s. 6d.

"*The pleasant companionship which Mrs. Macquoid offers, while wandering from one point of interest to another, seems to throw a renewed charm around each oft-depicted scene.*"—MORNING POST.

Crown 8vo, cloth extra, with Illustrations, 2s. 6d.

Madre Natura v. The Moloch of Fashion.

By LUKE LIMNER. With 32 Illustrations by the Author. FOURTH EDITION, revised and enlarged.

Handsomely printed in facsimile, price 5s.

Magna Charta.

An exact Facsimile of the Original Document in the British Museum, printed on fine plate paper, nearly 3 feet long by 2 feet wide, with the Arms and Seals emblazoned in Gold and Colours.

Small 8vo, 1s.; cloth extra, 1s. 6d.

Milton's The Hygiene of the Skin.

A Concise Set of Rules for the Management of the Skin ; with Directions for Diet, Wines, Soaps, Baths, &c. By J. L. MILTON, Senior Surgeon to St. John's Hospital.

BY THE SAME AUTHOR.

The Bath in Diseases of the Skin. Small 8vo, 1s.; cloth extra, 1s. 6d.

Mallock's (W. H.) Works:

Is Life Worth Living? By WILLIAM HURRELL MALLOCK. Demy 8vo, cloth extra, 12s. 6d.

" *This deeply interesting volume. . . . . It is the most powerful vindication of religion, both natural and revealed, that has appeared since Bishop Butler wrote, and is much more useful than either the Analogy or the Sermons of that great divine, as a refutation of the peculiar form assumed by the infidelity of the present day. . . . Deeply philosophical as the book is, there is not a heavy page in it. The writer is 'possessed,' so to speak, with his great subject, has sounded its depths, surveyed it in all its extent, and brought to bear on it all the resources of a vivid, rich, and impassioned style, as well as an adequate acquaintance with the science, the philosophy, and the literature of the day.*"—IRISH DAILY NEWS.

The New Republic; or, Culture, Faith, and Philosophy in an English Country House. By WILLIAM HURRELL MALLOCK. Crown 8vo, cloth extra, 6s. Also a CHEAP EDITION, in the "Mayfair Library," at 2s. 6d.

The New Paul and Virginia; or, Positivism on an Island. By WILLIAM HURRELL MALLOCK. Crown 8vo, cloth extra, 3s. 6d. Also a CHEAP EDITION, in the "Mayfair Library," at 2s. 6d.

Poems. By WILLIAM HURRELL MALLOCK. Small 4to, bound in parchment, 8s.

Mark Twain's Works:

The Choice Works of Mark Twain. Revised and Corrected throughout by the Author. With Life, Portrait, and numerous Illustrations. Crown 8vo, cloth extra, 7s. 6d.

The Adventures of Tom Sawyer. By MARK TWAIN. With One Hundred Illustrations. Small 8vo, cloth extra, 7s. 6d.

*** Also a CHEAP EDITION, in illustrated boards, at 2s.

" *A book to be read. There is a certain freshness and novelty about it, a practically romantic character, so to speak, which will make it very attractive.*"—SPECTATOR.

A Pleasure Trip on the Continent of Europe : The Innocents Abroad, and The New Pilgrim's Progress. By MARK TWAIN. Post 8vo, illustrated boards, 2s.

An Idle Excursion, and other Sketches. By MARK TWAIN. Post 8vo, illustrated boards, 2s.

A Tramp Abroad. By MARK TWAIN. Two Vols., cr. 8vo, 21s.

Small 8vo, cloth limp, with Illustrations, 2s. 6d.

Miller's Physiology for the Young;

Or, The House of Life: Human Physiology, with its Applications to the Preservation of Health. For use in Classes and Popular Reading. With numerous Illustrations. By Mrs. F. FENWICK MILLER.

"*An admirable introduction to a subject which all who value health and enjoy life should have at their fingers' ends.*"—ECHO.

Crown 8vo, cloth extra, with Frontispiece, 7s. 6d.

Moore's (Thos.) Prose and Verse—Humorous,

Satirical, and Sentimental. Including Suppressed Passages from the Memoirs of Lord Byron. Edited, by RICHARD HERNE SHEPHERD.

Post 8vo, cloth limp, 2s. 6d. per vol.

Mayfair Library, The:

The New Republic. By W. H. MALLOCK.

The New Paul and Virginia. By W. H. MALLOCK.

The True History of Joshua Davidson. By E. LYNN LINTON.

Old Stories Re-told. By WALTER THORNBURY.

Thoreau: His Life and Aims. By H. A. PAGE.

By Stream and Sea. By WILLIAM SENIOR.

Jeux d'Esprit. Edited by HENRY S. LEIGH.

Puniana. By the Hon. HUGH ROWLEY.

More Puniana. By the Hon. HUGH ROWLEY.

Puck on Pegasus. By H. CHOLMONDELEY-PENNELL.

Muses of Mayfair. Edited by H. CHOLMONDELEY-PENNELL.

Gastronomy as a Fine Art. By BRILLAT-SAVARIN.

Original Plays. By W. S. GILBERT.

Carols of Cockayne. By HENRY S. LEIGH.

⁎ *Other Volumes are in preparation.*

New Novels.

WILKIE COLLINS'S NEW NOVEL.

JEZEBEL'S DAUGHTER. By WILKIE COLLINS. Three Vols., crown 8vo.

"*The statement of the plot is in Mr. Wilkie Collins's best style. There is nothing irrelevant, the necessary facts are laid before the reader with the greatest clearness, and a point is artistically worked up to where one cannot help asking oneself what is to be the solution. Mr. Collins's work is altogether distinct from the novels of the day. He has the gift, which hardly any of his contemporaries possess in any degree, of inventing plots which are fascinating apart from personal interest in the characters.*"—ATHENÆUM.

NEW NOVEL BY MRS. LYNN LINTON.

WITH A SILKEN THREAD, and other Stories. By E. LYNN LINTON, Author of "Patricia Kemball," &c. Three Vols., crown 8vo. [*In the press.*

OUIDA'S NEW NOVEL.

PIPPISTRELLO, and other Stories. By OUIDA, Author of "Puck," "Ariadne," &c. One Vol., crown 8vo. [*In the press.*

CHARLES GIBBON'S NEW NOVEL.

ALL A GREEN WILLOW, and other Stories. By CHARLES GIBBON, Author of "Queen of the Meadow," &c. One vol., crown 8vo. [*In the press.*

NEW AND CHEAPER EDITION, crown 8vo, cloth extra, 6s.

UNDER ONE ROOF. By JAMES PAYN. [*In the press.*

Square 8vo, cloth extra, with numerous Illustrations, 9s.

North Italian Folk.
By Mrs. COMYNS CARR. Illustrated by RANDOLPH CALDECOTT.

"*A delightful book, of a kind which is far too rare. If anyone wants to really know the North Italian folk, we can honestly advise him to omit the journey, and sit down to read Mrs. Carr's pages instead. . . . Description with Mrs. Carr is a real gift. . . . It is rarely that a book is so happily illustrated.*"—CONTEMPORARY REVIEW.

Crown 8vo, cloth extra, with Vignette Portraits, price 6s. per Vol.

Old Dramatists, The:

Ben Jonson's Works.
With Notes, Critical and Explanatory, and a Biographical Memoir by WILLIAM GIFFORD. Edited by Colonel CUNNINGHAM. Three Vols.

Chapman's Works.
Now First Collected. Complete in Three Vols. Vol. I. contains the Plays complete, including the doubtful ones; Vol. II. the Poems and Minor Translations, with an Introductory Essay by ALGERNON CHARLES SWINBURNE. Vol. III. the Translations of the Iliad and Odyssey.

Marlowe's Works.
Including his Translations. Edited, with Notes and Introduction, by Col. CUNNINGHAM. One Vol.

Massinger's Plays.
From the Text of WILLIAM GIFFORD. With the addition of the Tragedy of "Believe as you List." Edited by Col. CUNNINGHAM. One Vol.

Crown 8vo, red cloth extra, 5s. each.

Ouida's Novels.—Library Edition.

Held in Bondage.	By OUIDA.	Folle Farine.	By OUIDA.
Strathmore.	By OUIDA.	Dog of Flanders.	By OUIDA.
Chandos.	By OUIDA.	Pascarel.	By OUIDA.
Under Two Flags.	By OUIDA.	Two Wooden Shoes.	By OUIDA.
Idalia.	By OUIDA.	Signa.	By OUIDA.
Cecil Castlemaine.	By OUIDA.	In a Winter City.	By OUIDA.
Tricotrin.	By OUIDA.	Ariadne.	By OUIDA.
Puck.	By OUIDA.	Friendship.	By OUIDA.

*** Also a Cheap Edition, post 8vo, illustrated boards, at 2s. each.

Post 8vo, cloth limp, 1s. 6d.

Parliamentary Procedure, A Popular Handbook of. By HENRY W. LUCY.

Crown 8vo, cloth extra, with Portrait and Illustrations, 7s. 6d.

Poe's Choice Prose and Poetical Works.
With BAUDELAIRE'S "Essay."

Crown 8vo, cloth extra, Illustrated, 7s. 6d.

Poe, The Life of Edgar Allan.
By W. F. GILL. With numerous Illustrations and Facsimiles.

Crown 8vo, carefully printed on creamy paper, and tastefully bound in cloth for the Library, price 6s. each.

Piccadilly Novels, The.
Popular Stories by the Best Authors.

READY-MONEY MORTIBOY. By W. Besant and James Rice.

MY LITTLE GIRL. By W. Besant and James Rice.

THE CASE OF MR. LUCRAFT. By W. Besant and James Rice.

THIS SON OF VULCAN. By W. Besant and James Rice.

WITH HARP AND CROWN. By W. Besant and James Rice.

THE GOLDEN BUTTERFLY. By W. Besant and James Rice. With a Frontispiece by F. S. Walker.

BY CELIA'S ARBOUR. By W. Besant and James Rice.

THE MONKS OF THELEMA. By W. Besant and James Rice.

'TWAS IN TRAFALGAR'S BAY. By W. Besant & James Rice.

ANTONINA. By Wilkie Collins. Illustrated by Sir J. Gilbert and Alfred Concanen.

BASIL. By Wilkie Collins. Illustrated by Sir John Gilbert and J. Mahoney.

HIDE AND SEEK. By Wilkie Collins. Illustrated by Sir John Gilbert and J. Mahoney.

THE DEAD SECRET. By Wilkie Collins. Illustrated by Sir John Gilbert and H. Furniss.

QUEEN OF HEARTS. By Wilkie Collins. Illustrated by Sir John Gilbert and A. Concanen.

MY MISCELLANIES. By Wilkie Collins. With Steel Portrait, and Illustrations by A. Concanen.

THE WOMAN IN WHITE. By Wilkie Collins. Illustrated by Sir J. Gilbert and F. A. Fraser.

THE MOONSTONE. By Wilkie Collins. Illustrated by G. Du Maurier and F. A. Fraser.

MAN AND WIFE. By Wilkie Collins. Illust. by Wm. Small.

POOR MISS FINCH. By Wilkie Collins. Illustrated by G. Du Maurier and Edward Hughes.

MISS OR MRS. ? By Wilkie Collins. Illustrated by S. L. Fildes and Henry Woods.

THE NEW MAGDALEN. By Wilkie Collins. Illustrated by G. Du Maurier and C. S. Reinhart.

THE FROZEN DEEP. By Wilkie Collins. Illustrated by G. Du Maurier and J. Mahoney.

THE LAW AND THE LADY. By Wilkie Collins. Illustrated by S. L. Fildes and Sydney Hall.

PICCADILLY NOVELS—*continued.*

OPEN! SESAME! By FLORENCE MARRYAT. Illustrated by F. A. FRASER.

TOUCH AND GO. By JEAN MIDDLEMASS.

WHITELADIES. By Mrs. OLIPHANT. With Illustrations by A. HOPKINS and H. WOODS.

THE BEST OF HUSBANDS. By JAMES PAYN. Illustrated by J. MOYR SMITH.

FALLEN FORTUNES. By JAMES PAYN.

HALVES. By JAMES PAYN. With a Frontispiece by J. MAHONEY.

WALTER'S WORD. By JAMES PAYN. Illust. by J. MOYR SMITH.

WHAT HE COST HER. By JAMES PAYN.

LESS BLACK THAN WE'RE PAINTED. By JAMES PAYN.

BY PROXY. By JAMES PAYN. Illustrated by ARTHUR HOPKINS.

HER MOTHER'S DARLING. By Mrs. J. H. RIDDELL.

BOUND TO THE WHEEL. By JOHN SAUNDERS.

GUY WATERMAN. By JOHN SAUNDERS.

ONE AGAINST THE WORLD. By JOHN SAUNDERS.

THE LION IN THE PATH. By JOHN SAUNDERS.

THE WAY WE LIVE NOW. By ANTHONY TROLLOPE. Illust.

THE AMERICAN SENATOR. By ANTHONY TROLLOPE.

DIAMOND CUT DIAMOND. By T. A. TROLLOPE.

Post 8vo, illustrated boards, 2s. each.

Popular Novels, Cheap Editions of.

[WILKIE COLLINS' NOVELS and BESANT and RICE'S NOVELS may also be had in cloth limp at 2s. 6d. See, too, the PICCADILLY NOVELS, *for Library Editions.*]

Maid, Wife, or Widow? By Mrs. ALEXANDER.

Ready-Money Mortiboy. By WALTER BESANT and JAMES RICE.

The Golden Butterfly. By Authors of "Ready-Money Mortiboy."

This Son of Vulcan. By the same.

My Little Girl. By the same.

The Case of Mr. Lucraft. By Authors of "Ready-Money Mortiboy."

With Harp and Crown. By Authors of "Ready-Money Mortiboy."

The Monks of Thelema. By WALTER BESANT and JAMES RICE.

By Celia's Arbour. By WALTER BESANT and JAMES RICE.

'Twas in Trafalgar's Bay. By WALTER BESANT and JAMES RICE.

Juliet's Guardian. By Mrs. H. LOVETT CAMERON.

Surly Tim. By F. H. BURNETT.

The Cure of Souls. By MACLAREN COBBAN.

The Woman in White. By WILKIE COLLINS.

Antonina. By WILKIE COLLINS.

Basil. By WILKIE COLLINS.

Hide and Seek. By the same.

POPULAR NOVELS—*continued.*

The Queen of Hearts. By WILKIE COLLINS.

The Dead Secret. By the same.

My Miscellanies. By the same.

The Moonstone. By the same.

Man and Wife. By WILKIE COLLINS.

Poor Miss Finch. By the same.

Miss or Mrs. ? By the same.

The New Magdalen. By WILKIE COLLINS.

The Frozen Deep. By the same.

The Law and the Lady. By WILKIE COLLINS.

The Two Destinies. By WILKIE COLLINS.

The Haunted Hotel. By WILKIE COLLINS.

Roxy. By EDWARD EGGLESTON.

Felicia. M. BETHAM-EDWARDS.

Filthy Lucre. By ALBANY DE FONBLANQUE.

Olympia. By R. E. FRANCILLON.

Dick Temple. By JAMES GREENWOOD.

Under the Greenwood Tree. By THOMAS HARDY.

An Heiress of Red Dog. By BRET HARTE.

The Luck of Roaring Camp. By BRET HARTE.

Gabriel Conroy. BRET HARTE.

Fated to be Free. By JEAN INGELOW.

The Queen of Connaught. By HARRIETT JAY.

The Dark Colleen. By HARRIETT JAY.

Number Seventeen. By HENRY KINGSLEY.

Oakshott Castle. By the same.

Patricia Kemball. By E. LYNN LINTON.

The Atonement of Leam Dundas By E. LYNN LINTON.

The World Well Lost. By E. LYNN LINTON.

The Waterdale Neighbours. By JUSTIN McCARTHY.

My Enemy's Daughter. By JUSTIN McCARTHY.

Linley Rochford. By the same.

A Fair Saxon. By the same.

Dear Lady Disdain. By the same.

Miss Misanthrope. By JUSTIN McCARTHY.

Lost Rose. By KATHARINE S. MACQUOID.

The Evil Eye. By KATHARINE S. MACQUOID.

Open! Sesame! By FLORENCE MARRYAT.

Whiteladies. Mrs. OLIPHANT.

Held in Bondage. By OUIDA.

Strathmore. By OUIDA.

Chandos. By OUIDA.

Under Two Flags. By OUIDA.

Idalia. By OUIDA.

Cecil Castlemaine. By OUIDA.

Tricotrin. By OUIDA.

Puck. By OUIDA.

Folle Farine. By OUIDA.

Dog of Flanders. By OUIDA.

Pascarel. By OUIDA.

Two Little Wooden Shoes. OUIDA.

Signa. By OUIDA.

In a Winter City. By OUIDA.

Ariadne. By OUIDA.

Fallen Fortunes. By J. PAYN.

Halves. By JAMES PAYN.

What He Cost Her. By ditto.

By Proxy. By JAMES PAYN.

Less Black than We're Painted. By JAMES PAYN.

The Best of Husbands. By JAMES PAYN.

POPULAR NOVELS—*continued.*

Walter's Word. By J. PAYN.

The Mystery of Marie Roget. By EDGAR A. POE.

Her Mother's Darling. By Mrs. J. H. RIDDELL.

Gaslight and Daylight. By GEORGE AUGUSTUS SALA.

Bound to the Wheel. By JOHN SAUNDERS.

Guy Waterman. J. SAUNDERS.

One Against the World. By JOHN SAUNDERS.

The Lion in the Path. By JOHN and KATHERINE SAUNDERS.

Tales for the Marines. By WALTER THORNBURY.

The Way we Live Now. By ANTHONY TROLLOPE.

The American Senator. By ANTHONY TROLLOPE.

Diamond Cut Diamond. By T. A. TROLLOPE.

An Idle Excursion. By MARK TWAIN.

Adventures of Tom Sawyer. By MARK TWAIN.

A Pleasure Trip on the Continent of Europe. By MARK TWAIN.

Fcap. 8vo, picture covers, 1s. each.

Jeff Briggs's Love Story. By BRET HARTE.

The Twins of Table Mountain. By BRET HARTE.

Mrs. Gainsborough's Diamonds. By JULIAN HAWTHORNE.

Kathleen Mavourneen. By the Author of "That Lass o' Lowrie's."

Lindsay's Luck. By the Author of "That Lass o' Lowrie's."

Pretty Polly Pemberton. By Author of "That Lass o' Lowrie's."

Trooping with Crows. By Mrs. PIRKIS.

Two Vols. 8vo, cloth extra, with Illustrations, 10s. 6d.

Plutarch's Lives of Illustrious Men.

Translated from the Greek, with Notes, Critical and Historical, and a Life of Plutarch, by JOHN and WILLIAM LANGHORNE. New Edition, with Medallion Portraits.

Crown 8vo, cloth extra, 7s. 6d.

Primitive Manners and Customs.

By JAMES A. FARRER.

"*A book which is really both instructive and amusing, and which will open a new field of thought to many readers.*"—ATHENÆUM.

"*An admirable example of the application of the scientific method and the working of the truly scientific spirit.*"—SATURDAY REVIEW.

Small 8vo, cloth extra, with Illustrations, 3s. 6d.

Prince of Argolis, The:

A Story of the Old Greek Fairy Time. By J. MOYR SMITH. With 130 Illustrations by the Author.

Crown 8vo, cloth extra, with Portrait and Facsimile, 7s. 6d.

Prout (Father), The Final Reliques of.

Collected and Edited, from MSS. supplied by the family of the Rev. FRANCIS MAHONY, by BLANCHARD JERROLD.

Proctor's (R. A.) Works:

Myths and Marvels of Astronomy. By RICH. A. PROCTOR, Author of "Other Worlds than Ours," &c. Demy 8vo, cloth extra, 12s. 6d.

Pleasant Ways in Science. By RICHARD A. PROCTOR. Crown 8vo, cloth extra, 10s. 6d.

Rough Ways made Smooth: A Series of Familiar Essays on Scientific Subjects. By RICHARD A. PROCTOR. Crown 8vo, cloth extra, 10s. 6d.

Our Place among Infinities: A Series of Essays contrasting our Little Abode in Space and Time with the Infinities Around us. By RICHARD A. PROCTOR. Crown 8vo, cloth extra, 6s.

The Expanse of Heaven: A Series of Essays on the Wonders of the Firmament. By RICHARD A. PROCTOR. Crown 8vo, cloth extra, 6s.

Wages and Wants of Science Workers. Showing the Resources of Science as a Vocation, and Discussing the Scheme for their Increase out of the National Exchequer. By RICHARD A. PROCTOR. Crown 8vo, 1s. 6d.

"Mr. Proctor, of all writers of our time, best conforms to Matthew Arnold's conception of a man of culture, in that he strives to humanise knowledge and divest it of whatever is harsh, crude, or technical, and so makes it a source of happiness and brightness for all."—WESTMINSTER REVIEW.

Crown 8vo, cloth extra, gilt, 7s. 6d.

Pursuivant of Arms, The;

or, Heraldry founded upon Facts. A Popular Guide to the Science of Heraldry. By J. R. PLANCHE, Somerset Herald. With Coloured Frontispiece, Plates, and 200 Illustrations.

Crown 8vo, cloth extra, with Illustrations, 7s. 6d.

Rabelais' Works.

Faithfully Translated from the French, with variorum Notes, and numerous characteristic Illustrations by GUSTAVE DORE.

" His buffoonery was not merely Brutus's rough skin, which contained a rod of gold: it was necessary as an amulet against the monks and legates; and he must be classed with the greatest creative minds in the world—with Shakespeare, with Dante, and with Cervantes."—S. T. COLERIDGE.

Crown 8vo, cloth gilt, with numerous Illustrations, and a beautifully executed Chart of the various Spectra, 7s. 6d.

Rambosson's Astronomy.

By J. RAMBOSSON, Laureate of the Institute of France. Translated by C. B. PITMAN. Profusely Illustrated.

Crown 8vo, cloth extra, with Illustrations, 7s. 6d.

Regalia: Crowns, Coronations, and Inaugura-

tions, in various Ages and Countries. By W. JONES, F.S.A., Author of "Finger-Ring Lore," &c. With very numerous Illustrations. *[In preparation.*

Crown 8vo, cloth extra, 10s. 6d,

Richardson's (Dr.) A Ministry of Health,

and other Papers. By BENJAMIN WARD RICHARDSON, M.D., &c.

"*This highly interesting volume contains upwards of nine addresses, written in the author's well-known style, and full of great and good thoughts. . . . The work is, like all those of the author, that of a man of genius, of great power, of experience, and noble independence of thought.*"—POPULAR SCIENCE REVIEW.

Handsomely printed, price 5s.

Roll of Battle Abbey, The ;

or, A List of the Principal Warriors who came over from Normandy with William the Conqueror, and Settled in this Country, A.D. 1066–7. Printed on fine plate paper, nearly three feet by two, with the principal Arms emblazoned in Gold and Colours.

Two Vols., large 4to, profusely Illustrated, half-morocco, £2 16s.

Rowlandson, the Caricaturist.

A Selection from his Works, with Anecdotal Descriptions of his Famous Caricatures, and a Sketch of his Life, Times, and Contemporaries. With nearly 400 Illustrations, mostly in Facsimile of the Originals. By JOSEPH GREGO, Author of "James Gillray, the Caricaturist; his Life, Works, and Times."

"*Mr. Grego's excellent account of the works of Thomas Rowlandson . . . illustrated with some 400 spirited, accurate, and clever transcripts from his designs. . . . The thanks of all who care for what is original and personal in art are due to Mr. Grego for the pains he has been at, and the time he has expended, in the preparation of this very pleasant, very careful, and adequate memorial.*"—PALL MALL GAZETTE.

Crown 8vo, cloth extra, profusely Illustrated, 4s. 6d. each.

"Secret Out" Series, The.

The Pyrotechnist's Treasury;
or, Complete Art of Making Fireworks. By THOMAS KENTISH. With numerous Illustrations.

The Art of Amusing :
A Collection of Graceful Arts, Games, Tricks, Puzzles, and Charades. By FRANK BELLEW. 300 Illustrations.

Hanky-Panky :
Very Easy Tricks, Very Difficult Tricks, White Magic, Sleight of Hand. Edited by W. H. CREMER. 200 Illustrations.

The Merry Circle :
A Book of New Intellectual Games and Amusements. By CLARA BELLEW. Many Illustrations.

Magician's Own Book :
Performances with Cups and Balls, Eggs, Hats, Handkerchiefs, &c. All from Actual Experience. Edited by W. H. CREMER. 200 Illustrations.

Magic No Mystery :
Tricks with Cards, Dice, Balls, &c., with fully descriptive Directions ; the Art of Secret Writing ; Training of Performing Animals, &c. Coloured Frontispiece and many Illustrations.

The Secret Out :
One Thousand Tricks with Cards, and other Recreations ; with Entertaining Experiments in Drawing-room or "White Magic." By W. H. CREMER. 300 Engravings.

Crown 8vo, cloth extra, 6s.

Senior's Travel and Trout in the Antipodes.

An Angler's Sketches in Tasmania and New Zealand. By WILLIAM SENIOR ("Red Spinner"), Author of "Stream and Sea."

"*In every way a happy production. . . . What Turner effected in colour on canvas, Mr. Senior may be said to effect by the force of a practical mind, in language that is magnificently descriptive, on his subject. There is in both painter and writer the same magical combination of idealism and realism, and the same hearty appreciation for all that is sublime and pathetic in natural scenery. That there is an undue share of travel to the number of trout caught is certainly not Mr. Senior's fault; but the comparative scarcity of the prince of fishes is adequately atoned for, in that the writer was led pretty well through all the glorious scenery of the antipodes in quest of him. . . . So great is the charm and the freshness and the ability of the book, that it is hard to put it down when once taken up.*"—HOME NEWS.

Shakespeare and Shakespeareana:

Shakespeare, The First Folio. Mr. WILLIAM SHAKESPEARE'S Comedies, Histories, and Tragedies. Published according to the true Originall Copies. London, Printed by ISAAC IAGGARD and ED. BLOUNT, 1623.—A Reproduction of the extremely rare original, in reduced facsimile by a photographic process—ensuring the strictest accuracy in every detail. Small 8vo, half-Roxburghe, 10s. 6d.

"*To Messrs. Chatto and Windus belongs the merit of having done more to facilitate the critical study of the text of our great dramatist than all the Shakespeare clubs and societies put together. A complete facsimile of the celebrated First Folio edition of 1623 for half-a-guinea is at once a miracle of cheapness and enterprise. Being in a reduced form, the type is necessarily rather diminutive, but it is as distinct as in a genuine copy of the original, and will be found to be as useful and far more handy to the student than the latter.*"—ATHENÆUM.

Shakespeare, The Lansdowne. Beautifully printed in red and black, in small but very clear type. With engraved facsimile of DROESHOUT's Portrait. Post 8vo, cloth extra, 7s. 6d.

Shakspere's Dramatic Works, Poems, Doubtful Plays, and Biography.—CHARLES KNIGHT'S PICTORIAL EDITION, with many hundred beautiful Engravings on Wood of Views, Costumes, Old Buildings, Antiquities, Portraits, &c. Eight Vols., royal 8vo, cloth extra, £3 12s.

Shakespeare for Children: Tales from Shakespeare. By CHARLES and MARY LAMB. With numerous Illustrations, coloured and plain, by J. MOYR SMITH. Crown 4to, cloth gilt, 10s. 6d.

Shakspere, The School of. Including "The Life and Death of Captain Thomas Stukeley," "Nobody and Somebody," "Histriomastix," "The Prodigal Son," "Jack Drum's Entertainment," "A Warning for Fair Women," and "Fair Em." Edited, with Notes, by RICHARD SIMPSON. Introduction by F. J. FURNIVALL. Two Vols., crown 8vo, cloth extra, 18s.

Shakespeare Music, The Handbook of. Being an Account of Three Hundred and Fifty Pieces of Music, set to Words taken from the Plays and Poems of Shakespeare, the compositions ranging from the Elizabethan Age to the Present Time. By ALFRED ROFFE. 4to, half-Roxburghe, 7s.

Shakespeare, A Study of. By ALGERNON CHARLES SWINBURNE. Crown 8vo, cloth extra, 8s.

Crown 8vo, cloth extra, gilt, with 10 full-page Tinted Illustrations, 7s. 6d.

Sheridan's Complete Works,

with Life and Anecdotes. Including his Dramatic Writings, printed from the Original Editions, his Works in Prose and Poetry, Translations, Speeches, Jokes, Puns, &c.; with a Collection of Sheridaniana.

Crown 8vo, cloth extra, with Illustrations, 7s. 6d.

Signboards :

Their History. With Anecdotes of Famous Taverns and Remarkable Characters. By JACOB LARWOOD and JOHN CAMDEN HOTTEN. With nearly 100 Illustrations.

"*Even if we were ever so maliciously inclined, we could not pick out all Messrs. Larwood and Hotten's plums, because the good things are so numerous as to defy the most wholesale depredation.*"—TIMES.

Crown 8vo, cloth extra, gilt, 6s. 6d.

Slang Dictionary, The:

Etymological, Historical, and Anecdotal. An ENTIRELY NEW EDITION, revised throughout, and considerably Enlarged.

"*We are glad to see the Slang Dictionary reprinted and enlarged. From a high scientific point of view this book is not to be despised. Of course it cannot fail to be amusing also. It contains the very vocabulary of unrestrained humour, and oddity, and grotesqueness. In a word, it provides valuable material both for the student of language and the student of human nature.*"—ACADEMY.

Exquisitely printed in miniature, cloth extra, gilt edges, 2s. 6d.

Smoker's Text-Book, The.

By J. HAMER, F.R.S.L.

Crown 8vo, cloth extra, 5s.

Spalding's Elizabethan Demonology :

An Essay in Illustration of the Belief in the Existence of Devils, and the Powers possessed by them, as it was generally held during the period of the Reformation, and the times immediately succeeding; with Special Reference to Shakspere and his Works. By T. ALFRED SPALDING, LL.B.

Crown 4to, uniform with "Chaucer for Children," with Coloured Illustrations, cloth gilt, 10s. 6d.

Spenser for Children.

By M. H. TOWRY. With Illustrations in Colours by WALTER J. MORGAN.

"*Spenser has simply been transferred into plain prose, with here and there a line or stanza quoted, where the meaning and the diction are within a child's comprehension, and additional point is thus given to the narrative without the cost of obscurity. . . . Altogether the work has been well and carefully done.*"—THE TIMES.

Crown 8vo, cloth extra, 9s.

Stedman's Victorian Poets :

Critical Essays. By EDMUND CLARENCE STEDMAN.

" We ought to be thankful to those who do critical work with competent skill and understanding, with honesty of purpose, and with diligence and thoroughness of execution. And Mr. Stedman, having chosen to work in this line, deserves the thanks of English scholars by these qualities and by something more ; . . . . he is faithful, studious, and discerning."—SATURDAY REVIEW.

Crown 8vo, cloth extra, with Illustrations, 7s. 6d.

Strutt's Sports and Pastimes of the People

of England ; including the Rural and Domestic Recreations, May Games, Mummeries, Shows, Processions, Pageants, and Pompous Spectacles, from the Earliest Period to the Present Time. With 140 Illustrations. Edited by WILLIAM HONE.

Crown 8vo, cloth extra, with Illustrations, 7s. 6d.

Swift's Choice Works,

In Prose and Verse. With Memoir, Portrait, and Facsimiles of the Maps in the Original Edition of "Gulliver's Travels."

Swinburne's Works :

The Queen Mother and Rosamond. Fcap. 8vo, 5s.

Atalanta in Calydon.
A New Edition. Crown 8vo, 6s.

Chastelard.
A Tragedy. Crown 8vo, 7s.

Poems and Ballads.
FIRST SERIES. Fcap. 8vo, 9s. Also in crown 8vo, at same price.

Poems and Ballads.
SECOND SERIES. Fcap. 8vo, 9s. Also in crown 8vo, at same price.

Notes on "Poems and Ballads." 8vo, 1s.

William Blake :
A Critical Essay. With Facsimile Paintings. Demy 8vo, 16s.

Songs before Sunrise.
Crown 8vo, 10s. 6d.

Bothwell :
A Tragedy. Crown 8vo, 12s. 6d.

George Chapman :
An Essay. Crown 8vo, 7s.

Songs of Two Nations.
Crown 8vo, 6s.

Essays and Studies.
Crown 8vo, 12s.

Erechtheus :
A Tragedy. Crown 8vo, 6s.

Note of an English Republican on the Muscovite Crusade. 8vo, 1s.

A Note on Charlotte Brontë.
Crown 8vo, 6s.

A Study of Shakespeare.
Crown 8vo, 8s.

NEW WORK BY MR. SWINBURNE.

Crown 8vo, cloth extra, 6s.

SONGS OF THE SPRING-TIDES. By ALGERNON C. SWINBURNE. *[In the press.*

Medium 8vo, cloth extra, with Illustrations, 7s.

Syntax's (Dr.) Three Tours,

in Search of the Picturesque, in Search of Consolation, and in Search of a Wife. With the whole of ROWLANDSON'S droll page Illustrations, in Colours, and Life of the Author by J. C. HOTTEN.

Four Vols. small 8vo, cloth boards, 30s.

Taine's History of English Literature.

Translated by HENRY VAN LAUN.

*** Also a POPULAR EDITION, in Two Vols. crown 8vo, cloth extra, 15s.

Crown 8vo, cloth gilt, profusely Illustrated, 6s.

Tales of Old Thule.

Collected and Illustrated by J. MOYR SMITH.

*"It is not often that we meet with a volume of fairy tales possessing more fully the double recommendation of absorbing interest and purity of tone than does the one before us containing a collection of 'Tales of Old Thule. These come, to say the least, near fulfilling the idea of perfect works of the kind ; and the illustrations with which the volume is embellished are equally excellent. . . . We commend the book to parents and teachers as an admirable gift to their children and pupils."—*LITERARY WORLD.

One Vol. crown 8vo, cloth extra, 7s. 6d.

Taylor's (Tom) Historical Dramas:

" Clancarty," " Jeanne Darc," " 'Twixt Axe and Crown," " The Fool's Revenge," " Arkwright's Wife," " Anne Boleyn," " Plot and Passion."

*** The Plays may also be had separately, at 1s. each.

Crown 8vo, cloth extra, with Coloured Frontispiece and numerous Illustrations, 7s. 6d.

Thackerayana :

Notes and Anecdotes. Illustrated by a profusion of Sketches by WILLIAM MAKEPEACE THACKERAY, depicting Humorous Incidents in his School-life, and Favourite Characters in the books of his every-day reading. With Hundreds of Wood Engravings, facsimiled from Mr. Thackeray's Original Drawings.

*"It would have been a real loss to bibliographical literature had copyright difficulties deprived the general public of this very amusing collection. One of Thackeray's habits, from his schoolboy days, was to ornament the margins and blank pages of the books he had in use with caricature illustrations of their contents. This gave special value to the sale of his library, and is almost cause for regret that it could not have been preserved in its integrity. Thackeray's place in literature is eminent enough to have made this an interest to future generations. The anonymous editor has done the best that he could to compensate for the lack of this. It is an admirable addendum, not only to his collected works, but also to any memoir of him that has been, or that is likely to be, written."—*BRITISH QUARTERLY REVIEW.

Crown 8vo, cloth extra, with numerous Illustrations, 7s. 6d.

Thornbury's (Walter) Haunted London.

A New Edition, edited by EDWARD WALFORD, M.A., with numerous Illustrations by F. W. FAIRHOLT, F.S.A.

*" Mr. Thornbury knew and loved his London. . . . He had read much history, and every by-lane and every court had associations for him. His memory and his note-books were stored with anecdote, and, as he had singular skill in the matter of narration it will be readily believed that when he took to writing a set book about the places he knew and cared for, the said book would be charming. Charming the volume before us certainly is. It may be begun in the beginning, or middle, or end, it is all one: wherever one lights, there is some pleasant and curious bit of gossip, some amusing fragment of allusion or quotation."—*VANITY FAIR.

Crown 8vo, cloth extra, gilt edges, with Illustrations, 7s. 6d.

Thomson's Seasons and Castle of Indolence.

With a Biographical and Critical Introduction by ALLAN CUNNING-HAM, and over 50 fine Illustrations on Steel and Wood.

Crown 8vo, cloth extra, with Illustrations, 7s. 6d.

Timbs' Clubs and Club Life in London.

With Anecdotes of its famous Coffee-houses, Hostelries, and Taverns. By JOHN TIMBS, F.S.A. With numerous Illustrations.

Crown 8vo, cloth extra, with Illustrations, 7s. 6d.

Timbs' English Eccentrics and Eccentrici-

ties: Stories of Wealth and Fashion, Delusions, Impostures, and Fanatic Missions, Strange Sights and Sporting Scenes, Eccentric Artists, Theatrical Folks, Men of Letters, &c. By JOHN TIMBS, F.S.A. With nearly 50 Illustrations.

Demy 8vo, cloth extra, 14s.

Torrens' The Marquess Wellesley,

Architect of Empire. An Historic Portrait. *Forming Vol. I. of* PROCONSUL and TRIBUNE: WELLESLEY and O'CONNELL: Historic Portraits. By W. M. TORRENS, M.P. In Two Vols.

Crown 8vo, cloth extra, with Coloured Illustrations, 7s. 6d.

Turner's (J. M. W.) Life and Correspondence:

Founded upon Letters and Papers furnished by his Friends and fellow-Academicians. By WALTER THORNBURY. A New Edition, considerably Enlarged. With numerous Illustrations in Colours, facsimiled from Turner's original Drawings.

Two Vols., crown 8vo, cloth extra, with Map and Ground-Plans, 14s.

Walcott's Church Work and Life in English

Minsters; and the English Student's Monasticon. By the Rev. MACKENZIE E. C. WALCOTT, B.D.

Large crown 8vo, cloth antique, with Illustrations, 7s. 6d.

Walton and Cotton's Complete Angler;

or, The Contemplative Man's Recreation: being a Discourse of Rivers. Fishponds, Fish and Fishing, written by IZAAK WALTON; and Instructions how to Angle for a Trout or Grayling in a clear Stream, by CHARLES COTTON. With Original Memoirs and Notes by Sir HARRIS NICOLAS, and 61 Copperplate Illustrations.

Carefully printed on paper to imitate the Original, 22 in. by 14 in., 2s.

Warrant to Execute Charles I.

An exact Facsimile of this important Document, with the Fifty-nine Signatures of the Regicides, and corresponding Seals.

The 20th Annual Edition, for 1880, elegantly bound, cloth, full gilt, price 50s.

Walford's County Families of the United

Kingdom.   A Royal Manual of the Titled and Untitled Aristocracy of Great Britain and Ireland. By EDWARD WALFORD, M.A., late Scholar of Balliol College, Oxford.   Containing Notices of the Descent, Birth, Marriage, Education, &c., of more than 12,000 distinguished Heads of Families in the United Kingdom, their Heirs Apparent or Presumptive, together with a Record of the Patronage at their disposal, the Offices which they hold or have held, their Town Addresses, Country Residences, Clubs, &c.

*" What would the gossips of old have given for a book which opened to them the recesses of every County Family in the Three Kingdoms ? . . . This work, however, will serve other purposes besides those of mere curiosity, envy, or malice. It is just the book for the lady of the house to have at hand when making up the County dinner, as it gives exactly that information which punctilious and particular people are so desirous of obtaining—the exact standing of every person in the county. To the business man, ' The County Families' stands in the place of directory and biographical dictionary. The fund of information it affords respecting the Upper Ten Thousand must give it a place in the lawyer's library ; and to the money-lender, who is so interested in finding out the difference between a gentleman and a ' gent,' between heirs-at-law and younger sons, Mr. Walford has been a real bene-factor.   In this splendid volume he has managed to meet a universal want—one which cannot fail to be felt by the lady in her drawing-room, the peer in his library, the tradesman in his counting-house, and the gentleman in his club."—*TIMES.

Beautifully printed on paper to imitate the Original MS., price 2s.

Warrant to Execute Mary Queen of Scots.

An exact Facsimile, including the Signature of Queen Elizabeth, and a Facsimile of the Great Seal.

Crown 8vo, cloth limp, with numerous Illustrations, 4s. 6d.

Westropp's Handbook of Pottery and Porce-

lain ; or, History of those Arts from the Earliest Period. By HODDER M. WESTROPP, Author of "Handbook of Archæology," &c. With numerous beautiful Illustrations, and a List of Marks.

SEVENTH EDITION.   Square 8vo, 1s.

Whistler v. Ruskin : Art and Art Critics.

By J. A. MACNEILL WHISTLER.

Crown 8vo, cloth extra, with Illustrations, 7s. 6d.

Wright's Caricature History of the Georges.

(The House of Hanover.) With 400 Pictures, Caricatures, Squibs, Broadsides, Window Pictures, &c. By THOMAS WRIGHT, M.A., F.S.A.

Large post 8vo, cloth extra, gilt, with Illustrations, 7s. 6d.

Wright's History of Caricature and of the

Grotesque in Art, Literature, Sculpture, and Painting, from the Earliest Times to the Present Day. By THOMAS WRIGHT, M.A., F.S.A.   Profusely Illustrated by F. W. FAIRHOLT, F.S.A.

J. OGDEN AND CO., PRINTERS, 172, ST. JOHN STREET, E.C.